Oleander

PRIDEFUL MAGICK COLLECTION
BOOK TWO

TENTH ANNIVERSARY EDITION

HOLLOW RYAN

Oleander

Second Edition

Published by Hollow Ryan

Ebook ISBN: 978-1-968729-04-2
Trade Paperback ISBN: 978-1-968729-03-5
Hardcover ISBN: 978-1-968729-05-9

Cover elements courtesy of:
Vintage Damask by DarkMoon_Art via Pixabay.com
Realistic Smoke Fog by Hakan Kaçar via Vecteezy.com
Flower Nature Herb by Konevi via Pixabay.com

Cover Design by Christiana Nehmsmann
Interior Design by Christiana Nehmsmann

Books By Hollow Ryan

Prideful Magick Collection

Ivy

Oleander

Valerian

Hawthorn

Avens

Demon Kin

Demon Kin: The Queen

Demon Kin: The Lovers

TABLE OF CONTENTS

For Mandy

The one always pushing me to be a better writer, and helping her friends to be better readers.

Chapter One

TRUTH

"The Defense calls Alexandria Ryder to the stand."

I tried to convince myself that I was prepared for this, while my heart tried to hammer its way out of my ribcage. The pounding of my pulse sounded like tribal drums in my ears as adrenaline flooded my bloodstream. Fight or flight?

My legs were unsteady underneath me and I locked my knees as soon as I stood up. Taking a deep breath, I forced one foot in front of the other as I crossed the open space in front of the jury. When I made it to the witness stand, I stepped up in front of the chair and raised my right hand as instructed.

"Do you swear to tell the truth, the whole

truth, and nothing but the truth?"

"I do."

"You may be seated."

It took every inch of willpower I had not to fall into that chair. When I was seated, I made sure to keep both feet firmly on the floor to keep my knee from bouncing. As I took in this new view of the courtroom, I found that I wasn't nearly as prepared as I had thought.

Surreal. It shouldn't have seemed that way, but it was. Like it could have been happening in a dream, or to someone else. How could this be happening to me?

The lawyer approached, her light hair gathered in a bun at the back of her head, jade eyes filled with purpose whilst her expression remained free of her thoughts. "Please state your name and age for the court." It wasn't a question.

"Alexandria Ryder. Fourteen."

I didn't realize how difficult it was to breathe until I had to speak. For one, long second, I took a deep breath and held it. When I exhaled, I tried to force all of the nerves out at the same time. It helped a little.

"Miss Ryder, why are you testifying here

today?"

"I want people to know the truth."

"Couldn't they learn it by the evidence being presented or the other statements presented?"

"No."

"Why not?"

The way she spoke was calm and inquisitive. Far from our first encounter with one another. Much had occurred since that day, and I found her presence more soothing than frustrating. Which was why the last of my nerves vanished as we talked, forgetting everything around us and what it meant in the long run.

"There are a dozen ways to interpret evidence. I've seen it firsthand in this very courtroom. What cannot be misinterpreted, however, is what I saw. Felt. Experienced. I know what happened, because I was there. Since the evidence can't say it plain, it's up to me to tell everyone what happened."

Her blue-green eyes narrowed in warning. In a voice laden with false suspicion, she demanded, "Why should we believe you?"

There is a fine line between truth and magick.

If every person in that room knew anything about magick, they would no longer know what was truth or lie. Illusion or revelation. Should any person come to know that everything I said was possible, they would no longer believe in the impossible.

They would never believe that it was impossible for me to murder someone I loved.

"I have no reason to lie."

"There are those that would beg to differ."

"They're wrong."

"Then prove it. Tell us what happened. Make us believe you."

Even as her words settled into my skin, a white mist rose up before my eyes, taking me back to this day one year ago.

Chapter Two

SUMMER BLOOMS

I laughed a little as the sloppy braid slid over my left shoulder once more. Shaking it out of the way, I tried not to lose the flow of the music as my fingers danced over the ivory keys of the grand piano. After four years of constant practice, I would never reach Juilliard standards, but I was more than adequate. According to my teacher, I was also one of the few students with the tenacity to stick it out for as long as I had. It was the polite way of saying that I was too stubborn to admit that I wouldn't improve beyond my current skill.

The grandfather clock in the doorway struck four in the afternoon, causing my smile to broaden. It was the first day of summer vacation. Like any other entitled teenager, I'd slept in until eleven and had a nice brunch the minute I'd awoken. After a shower, I'd thrown on an adorable sundress and one of those tiny, white, crocheted little pull-on things that barely covered the shoulders and were used for the sole purpose of looking cute. Adding my flip-flops, I'd hurried down to commit myself to the mandatory two-hour practice session I had set for myself. At last, it was over.

Leaping from the bench, I rushed to the kitchen where my mother was preparing snacks for her new book club. One day into vacation and she had already plotted a weekly activity. Of course, the club was mostly made up of her co-workers that didn't have lives outside of the school and had summers of nothingness awaiting them.

"Mom, I'm going to Morgan's," I announced before turning on my heel. I'd stashed my purse in the closet under the stairs. Grabbing that, I was soon out the front door and striding around to the shed.

My thoughts were guarded as I made the roundabout trip to the back of the three-storied brick house. The red stone was covered in green ivy splashed with red that reached for the heavens. It was carefully trimmed away from the windows and doorways, though I allowed the vines to once more hide the gothic-arched door that had been the site of much commotion only a few short years ago. Back when we first moved to Cedar Creek.

Not once since that fateful day when I had found the body of Alyssa Mae Rice, did I ever talk about it. Through numerous methods of searching, I had finally found the reason for the young girl's disappearance back in 1922. Never would I relive that day.

Pausing at the shed, my eyes trailed to the third-floor attic window. The window that had been a source of so much mystery that it was hard to believe that no one else took note. Shaking my head, I threw my leg over the seat and pushed down on the pedal. My mother would be so irritated if she knew I was biking in a dress, but I didn't care.

I rode the bike up to the gate. As I got off to open it and push it through, I looked back at my house once more.

This is how a house in New England should look.

They were the same words I thought the first time I'd stood at this gate, looking at my new home.

Four years was a long time to be in one place considering my dad was a Marine and liked to travel. Were it not for my obvious attachment to this house, I think he might have picked us up and moved us years ago. After my 'childhood trauma' of finding Alyssa, however, he was more worried about setting me off any which way. Shaking my head, I couldn't help but think, *If he only knew.*

Getting up on my bike again, I turned left. Verity Lane met up with Norfolk Street where I turned right. It would have been easier just to cross the road and take the trail through the woods, but I was too full of pride to go biking through the woods while looking so cute.

Like a flower that unfurls its petals with the spring morning, I had bloomed just before the summer. After already acting twice my age, I now looked a little closer to fourteen or fifteen than a girl who had just turned thirteen a few months past.

As can be imagined, my Ryder Pride was on a fantastic peak by this time.

Well, it would be if any of the guys my age would look twice at me.

Yet, of all the guys I'd gone to school with over the last four years, only one even acknowledged me. The others stayed clear. They wanted nothing to do with the girl that found a body and then refused to talk about it. Other girls then refused to befriend me after the whole 'she hangs out at the witch's house' story came out. I blamed Nathan's brother for that one. Nathan was the only person who knew, until his brother, Tyler, had actually grown the balls to come to Morgan's to deliver her mail when Nathan had been sick with the flu a few weeks ago.

Breathing out all of the negative thoughts, I made the right turn onto Old Grove Road. I'd been here so often that my bicycle tracks were practically embedded in the soil. I traveled this road more often than anyone else.

Except today.

As I reached Morgan's house, a raucous group of boys whirled by on their bikes, calling out derisive words at me. I turned to watch them with a raised eyebrow and a small smile. It bothered them when I did that. Before, I used to glare and wish I could curse them, but the karmic backfire from that would hit me times three. Instead, I just made them think that's what I was doing. Smiling at them was the only surefire way to get them to feel paranoid.

By this time, all of the other guys had looked back at me uneasily and sped up. However, there was one who seemed confused by all the names and how the others reacted to me. That boy kept glancing back at me and I felt an unfamiliar sense of unease run through me. Not something I'd experienced since the Alyssa days.

"His name is Matthew Graham. Moved here from California a few days ago. Guess you're not the new kid in school anymore," a somewhat familiar voice said at my shoulder.

I'd sensed the determined aura surrounding him and hadn't been taken by surprise. Turning to Nathan, I held my hand out for Morgan's mail. He handed it over wordlessly.

Four years. Four years of sitting side by side on the bus, at lunch, even in classes, and Nathan's voice was only somewhat familiar to me. I liked it that way. For us, there was a camaraderie in the silence. Zero expectations, but all of the comfort of knowing someone else was there for you if needed.

"And I care because...?"

Nathan raised an eyebrow at me. "Tomorrow shopping day?"

I nodded. "I'll join you tomorrow."

"See ya then," Nathan stated before getting on his bike. Pedaling fast, he followed the boys to the lake where they would go swimming.

Rolling my eyes, but glad to know the new kid's name, I patted the gargoyles, unlatched the gate, and stepped over the salt line. As I did almost every day.

Chapter Three

TENSION IN THE AIR

The moment I was over the negative-barring line, the strained atmosphere radiating from the house hit me like a cannon ball. The tension surrounding the place was even dragging the plants under some sort of spell of depression. Plants hated negativity. They were the most sensitive to its vibrations.

Another strangeness was the cats. Morgan partnered with six cats total. One was missing from the group sitting by the front door. Her Familiar was inside with her, helping the situation as well as he was able. My Familiar, the jade-eyed beauty that had claimed me my first day of school, now slunk over to me. She was in a terrible mood and my own mood rippled with hers. We affected each other like only witch and Familiar were able.

It took a fraction of a second for these things to register. Already my mind was settling itself into an empty state and I grounded and centered on instinct alone. My magick reached out, seeking the voices beyond the door while I was still standing at the gate.

Clairaudience. That was the ability to hear things normally indistinguishable by other people. Usually it meant the voices of the dead, but I had no problems communicating with them. It was hearing what the living had to say that provoked me into using this ability now.

"Does the girl know?" demanded a voice I was unfamiliar with.

"No."

"And the other children? My daughter?" the voice cracked as she tried to dig for information.

"They do not know me, for none will come near this house. Next to Nathan, Alexandria, alone, has been so brave. Your daughter has never shown an interest; nor the talent." Morgan added the last to fight fire with fire, I knew, but even from the gate, I could feel the ache that statement cost her.

I heard an audible, relieved sigh from the other woman as the fight seemed to drain out of her. "What have you done? How could you do this to her?"

"I have done only what was requested of me, Faylin. Alexandria knew the risks of what she was asking."

"She is a child! The risks are far greater than she realizes."

"No, they are not. Faylin, Alexandria has seen more than either of us could have imagined. The risks posed by her classmates hold little for her to fear compared to what else she has encountered," Morgan assured the woman.

"What has happened? What has she seen?" Even as irate as she was, Faylin couldn't help but be curious. As was the rest of the town.

"Things I am not at liberty to discuss."

"You weren't at liberty to train another, but you did that with no pressing at all," Faylin growled. A moment later, she added, "Of all the things I thought of you, I never pegged you as an oath breaker."

My curiosity piqued even as Morgan snarled, "Do not dare to insinuate such things, child. I have kept my word to the letter. The oath I made to your sister binds me still from forcing the Craft unto a being unwilling to learn. Alexandria has never been unwilling, however, and she blossoms each day as her powers grow."

"There's no difference between force and co-ercion, *Mother*. You and I should know that best of all. And while the girl came to you of her own accord, I have no doubt that your encouragement was all that was needed to start her down this path. One which you know will end with that little girl ostracized and alone. Is that really what you want for her?"

I had heard enough. My stomach churned with my repressed fury as I stormed toward the cottage. It had been one thing to show concern for my well-being, which I could hear was an honest emotion in Faylin's voice. However, it was quite another to insult Morgan and then accuse her of manipulating me. And I wasn't about to let her continue to discuss me with the woman who had become like my grandmother.

Throwing open the door, I glided into the silent room and went to stand behind where Morgan sat in the rocking chair. Careful to keep my hands from the familiar wood, I lifted my chin and stared at the woman who stood beside the fireplace.

"I did come to Morgan of my own accord. With all of the curiosity and enthusiasm of a nine-year-old who had begun to see ghosts. Morgan didn't coerce me into anything; she merely answered my questions. As for being ostracized, that was already in motion. I have far too much pride for those my age, and they've disliked me for it from the moment of my arrival. That isn't going to change, and it had nothing to do with Morgan. You forget: it is easiest for some people to be alone."

Faylin had done a fine job of keeping an impassive expression on her face when I'd come in, yet it had degenerated into a 'mom look' by the time I had finished speaking. Not the stern, hell-hath-no-fury face, but the 'you don't know enough yet' expression. It was beyond infuriating.

"You say that now–"

"And I have lived it my whole life. This is not my first town nor the first time I've been disconnected from the kids my age. I have always been like this, and I always will be. I don't need to see the future to know what is in store for me. My decisions have been made and I know what my life will hold."

My passionate words had no effect on her, I could see. Faylin shook her head in a way that spoke her feelings loud and clear. She didn't believe me, nor did I believe her. Just because it took her longer to figure out what would happen in her life, did not mean I was that blind.

Looking back to Morgan, Faylin gave her mother a rueful smile. "Was I so young once?"

"Yes," my friend answered.

"Fair enough." Turning her gaze back to me, I now got the stern mother look. "Contrary to popular belief, Alexandria, you will never know what the future has in store for you. Even if you are blessed with the gift of foresight. Think this through before you continue down this path. Others will not be so kind to you once they realize what you are capable of."

My chin raised a little as she walked past me. "And what is that?"

Pausing in the doorway, Faylin cast a sad smile in my direction. "Magick."

A stone settled in my stomach as the word came out a sentence rather than as reverence. It was a foreshadowing in and of itself, now that people knew what I was. What would others say or do once they realized the whole of my abilities? It was a question I had never pondered, even when my afternoon whereabouts had become common knowledge. Yet, what I had said was true: I had always been alone, and that wasn't about to change.

Once she was gone, I turned my gaze to Morgan. The aching in her heart called out to me, suggesting I soothe it away by whatever means necessary. Something I knew better than to attempt. Human beings needed sorrow just as much as they required joy. It was the balance of the world, and so I dared not impede on Morgan's.

Instead, I stepped more fully into her line of vision and smiled in as gentle a way as I could before saying, "So, you have daughters."

Though it hadn't been a question, Morgan gave a slow nod. "Yes."

Chapter Four

NERVOUS

"Will you tell me about them?" I knew the answer before I'd asked the question.

"No."

"Because their lives are their story and you will respect their wishes and not discuss their lives with someone they don't even know. I understand." A small smile turned up the corners of my mouth.

"Have I told you lately how happy I am to have you here?" Morgan teased.

"Not today. What do you say we go out in the garden and fix those plants? Faylin made a mess of them," I suggested.

"Well, I am happy that you're here. And that sounds like a terrific idea, my dear."

"I know."

Smiling, we both went outside into the daylight. Working in the garden, even in a dress, was a pleasing experience as I helped with the flowers. The Blood of Hestia smelled good and we collected some of the leaves in order to make chamomile tea. Sea Dew we picked some of in order to cook with. Rosemary chicken was fantastic when cooked with magick. At least, I thought so. Then there was the one flower I was never allowed to touch: oleander. My eyes drifted over it in welcome speculation, since it served no other purpose other than to look beautiful and be lethal.

"I didn't realize how late it was getting," Morgan announced almost two hours later, standing up and looking to the sundial.

"It's nowhere near sunset, yet."

"Yes, but you remember our agreement?"

I sighed.

Our agreement had been made at the end of the school year. I would sleep at home every night except for when Morgan asked me to stay for ceremonies. Sunset would be my marker to go home. The last requirement really bothered me:

balance both worlds. That meant that whenever Morgan deemed it necessary, I was to go and waste time out in 'the real world' with kids my age. Which also meant I was not to step foot near her house on the weekends–except in the case of a ceremony.

"Where will I go?"

"Nathan seemed to be heading toward the water. Perhaps you should join him."

"Ha! And deal with the pests gone ahead of him?" My tone was derisive.

"Yes."

"I'd rather go home and read a book," I muttered.

"It can't be that bad, Alexandria. Remember what you were taught. Visualize the outcome, then live it."

"I visualize this evening going by *very* quickly," I remarked as I washed my hands in the sink.

"Then I hope your visualizations prove fruitful," she chuckled.

Shooting a mock-glare over my shoulder, I accused, "You enjoy this way too much."

"You enjoy this way too little. Don't most teenagers enjoy taking time away from their studies in order to see people their own age?"

"Most do. I don't. I guess I will see you later," I sighed, managing to smile at her a little.

Morgan smiled as well. "Goodbye, my dear. I shall see you tomorrow."

Waving, I walked out of the door. Soil was still on my knees, I had a smudge on my nose, and my braid was frayed. I was now a mess. And I didn't care.

"Alex?" Nathan asked in surprise.

I smiled and waved grudgingly. "She sent me away early."

Nathan nodded and I continued walking. When I reached the edge of the water, I slipped off my flip-flops and eased into the cool liquid with my eyes closed.

I saw it every time I came here. Victoria's black hair flowing down her back. The Coven standing around her with baby Morgan in Alice's arms. Alice, who saw so much of the truth that only she knew what had happened between Victoria and Alyssa. Every time I came here, I pushed it so far from my mind that it disappeared into the depths of the lake. Just like Victoria.

Before I opened my eyes, the uneasiness swept over me once more. I took a deep breath and eased open my eyelids. Staring straight out over the water, I said, "You stole my title. I'm not the new kid in school anymore. Weird, considering I've been here for four years now."

"How'd you know I was here?" Matt asked, confused.

I turned to smile sardonically at him. "I have senses. I heard you coming. I felt the air change. And my instincts don't seem particularly fond of you. I am uneasy whenever you look at me."

"That's kinda weird," he informed me.

I shrugged and turned back to look over the lake. "Only to people who don't know how to trust their senses."

"Does that make it even weirder that I feel strange whenever *you* look at *me*?"

"Not to me," I replied with a smile. "So, we each make each other nervous. Interesting."

"What's funny is that I feel like I should stay away from you. But I'm too curious to walk away."

Turning my head back to him, I *really* looked

at Matt.

Brown hair swept across his forehead, looking shaggy and unkempt to me. Dark brown eyes were framed by gorgeous lashes. Matt had thin lips but a broad jaw, giving him as much of an older look as I had. At the same time, I was suddenly sure that he had a year in age on me.

"I suddenly feel the same way," I stated, confusion entering my voice. "What are you so curious about? And please do *not* say Alyssa Rice."

"Who?"

Right then, a huge weight fell away from me. Matt hadn't heard the story yet. He didn't have the time to jump to some messed up opinion of me. I wasn't the odd death mute that was so traumatized by her experience as a kid to talk to anyone about it.

"Nobody. Why are you so curious about me? I'm nobody special," I remarked.

"Not according to them," Matt said, pointing his chin in the direction of the other kids. Most were watching with avid interest and I rolled my eyes.

"And what have they to say about me?" I asked, wading further into the water until it covered my knees. Another inch and it would reach my dress.

"They said you were a witch and that you spent your time learning from the witch on Old Grove Road." Matt's tone was bland. Like he didn't care. Or, probably, he didn't believe them.

"That is the rumor." I shrugged once more as though it were no big deal.

"Personally, I don't believe in magic," Matt informed me.

I couldn't help looking up at him and smiling widely. The dimple in my left cheek became clear and Matt smiled back. He thought I was in agreement with him.

"It's cute that you think that," I remarked in almost too harsh of a voice. I was going to lose his positive interest anyway. Might as well get it over with.

"Why do you say that?" He was confused once more.

"Magick is everywhere, Matt. It is in everything and makes up everyone. It's just easier for some of us to work with it than others."

"People like you?"

"Yes," I answered simply. There went my 'she's

not a witch' status. Oh well. I had too much Ryder Pride to lie about what I was. It was a real good thing that my parents never asked me straight out if I was a witch.

"So, they were telling the truth?" Matt's voice was very skeptical.

"That I am a witch and continue to study under the woman down Old Grove Road? Yes. Are you afraid?" I made my voice teasing as Matt's eyes widened.

"No," he scoffed. "Knowing doesn't make me any more nervous than before. And I'm not sure I believe you. But you're definitely interesting."

My eyebrows rose and I couldn't help the surprised expression covering my face. "You're kidding me, right?" I managed to ask, my mouth hanging open.

Matt chuckled. "I'm not kidding. I'm still just as curious as before. Maybe even a little more so, now. You'd think having *that* for an answer would just make me walk away, but nope."

"Huh. You would think," I muttered in an amazed tone of voice.

"You've never had anybody come up and talk to you about it before, have you?" Matt asked in a sardonic voice. I shook my head, causing him to laugh a little.

"No. They secretly like that there's such a mystery in town. It gives them a kick knowing that they wander the halls with me and that I disappear into the witch's cottage on Old Grove Road. I'm a bit of an attraction. Like in a freak show. The only thing they would like more was if I dressed in black and cast spells on the teachers," I replied, rolling my eyes.

Matt laughed again and this time I laughed with him. Then someone called his name and we both turned to look back at the stunned group of kids.

"Well, Alex, I guess I better get going."

"Yeah. Don't want to give the scaredy cats a heart attack," I teased.

"Yeah," he replied. "It was nice to meet you, Alex."

"And it was nice to meet you, Matt. Thank you for talking to me."

Matt grinned at me and waved a little before meeting up with the others. I waved back. As he reached them I could almost hear their barrage of questions. For the first time, I felt like I was missing out on what was being said of me. But I didn't regret not eavesdropping on the conversation. I didn't want to know what Matt was telling them about me. I probably wouldn't like it.

"Well you look ... chipper." My mother had paused in the making of her fruit pizza in order to stare at me.

I continued smiling and walked over to the bowl of strawberries before stealing one and taking a bite. As casually as I could manage, I asked, "Is Dad home?"

"Not yet." She sounded skeptical and I couldn't hold it in any longer.

"I met a boy today. And he actually made me nervous."

My mother's face lit up like I hadn't seen it in the past four years. Ever since the Alyssa wall went up between us, we hadn't been as close as before. She was so ... peeved that I hadn't opened up to her about that experience. It had opened a small chasm between us; especially when my father took my side. Now she felt like she could be a part of my life again.

"A boy, hmm?"

I almost laughed at how hard she was trying to play off how interested she was. But I could tell that she was brimming with excitement. After all, this was mother/daughter stuff only.

"Yeah. He's new. From California."

"And does the boy from California have a name?" Mom laughed at me.

"Matthew Graham. We didn't talk much. It was just nice to have someone *talk* to me. And not like I was the freak of Cedar Creek."

"Baby, you're not a freak."

I had to shove away the uneasiness she felt. It was an emotion that I picked up on more than any others when it came to her. Living with the knowledge that someone was in a constant state of worry was more than a little tiring. Some days it was almost unbearable to be around her.

"Yeah, I know that," I said, trying to steer the subject back to Matt. "But a *boy* didn't think I was a freak. At least, he wasn't totally put off by my brashness. And, Mom, the best part: he made me *nervous*."

My mother laughed aloud. "How is that the best part?"

I gave her a 'seriously?' look. "Mom, when does *anything* make me nervous? When am I ever surprised by anything? What honestly affects me anymore? *Matt makes me nervous!* And I make him nervous, too."

"You're really excited about this," my mom noted, studying me with a new expression.

"Yeah. Yeah, I am. Four years being whispered about and teased and made fun of. All of that I've handled and ignored and shrugged off. Fine. But someone talked to me today and he had no idea who Alyssa Rice was. I mean, he probably knows the whole thing now. But the point is that he met me and talked to me first. I am just so glad that he talked to me first."

"I'm happy for you, Lex. Really happy."

She was more than happy. She was relieved. I could tell she was thinking that maybe now I would get to be a normal kid again. Poor Mom. She didn't know what I was. Although, I hadn't felt this normal ... ever.

Chapter Five

SIMILARITIES

I woke up with that strange butterfly feeling in my midsection and a small smile worked its way onto my face. To think that a boy made me feel this way, instead of magick, was hard enough to accept. Realizing that I sort-of had both was a little too much to comprehend.

Still smiling, I eased out of the bed and stretched. Without even looking, I used my magick to make the bed. The closet door swung open of its own accord and clothes started to drift out on hangers as I tried to make a decision. In the mornings, walking into my room was like walking onto the set of a witch movie. I regretted nothing.

After studying the outfits, I dismissed them all as too formal and not fun enough. When that happened, dresser drawers started to open and new selections were presented. In the end, I chose my blue bathing suit-a one piece since my dad wouldn't let me own a bikini before I was fifteen-a pair of cut-off blue jean shorts and a tank top. Once I'd made my decision, I prepared to get in the shower, grabbing a jar of dried alyssum and removing one of the plants.

Alyssum was a plant used for protection and anger management. Every morning I made sure to rub some on me in the shower. It would help to keep the awful things people said from affecting me. I didn't want to know how I would react without it.

As soon as I was ready, I headed downstairs to have breakfast with my parents. Of course, that turned into my mother soon enough. Dad had to work and left almost as soon as I walked into the kitchen. Mom practically beamed at me the moment he was gone.

"What are your plans today?" she asked in a hinting tone.

I grinned. "First I'm going grocery shopping for Morgan. Then I think I'm going to hang out with her for a while before going swimming."

"When do you plan on doing this?" she asked with a sly smile. Immediately I picked up on what she was smirking about.

"Right after I finish my practice session."

I finished my breakfast with a grin, took care of my plate, and walked into the parlor. With a smile, I sat at the piano and placed my fingers accordingly.

Something's going to happen, I thought to myself. It was easy to tell when magick and real life were about to collide. For me, it was easiest when magick often sent me warnings. Like now.

My fingers moved over the keyboard in a haunting, distressing lullaby. It might have been soothing to anyone but me. Of course, the only time I'd ever played it before was due to being possessed. And the only other times I heard it played were in my psychometric visions. It was Victoria's Lullaby. And it was a warning that *something* was going to happen today.

When the two hours were up, I once more jumped to my feet and called to my mother that I was going to Morgan's. Then I grabbed my backpack and headed out.

Stopping just beside my bike, I let my mind

trail ahead. Seeing the future was always a bit difficult for me. Especially when I was getting specific. But it got easier when I used the same focus and asked the same question. Things that wouldn't change too often in the next twenty-four hours. Like: What time would Nathan be at Morgan's? The answer: fifteen to noon. It was already eleven thirty. Good thing it wouldn't take me long to get to Morgan's. I'd arrive at about the same time Nathan did.

Jumping on my bike, I pedaled down the driveway this time, instead of bothering with the gate. Turning left and heading for Norfolk Street, I still possessed too much pride to go through the woods.

Sure enough, I made it to the corner of Old Grove Road and Norfolk Street at the same time Nathan did. Smiling slightly to him, we both continued down to Morgan's house, where she would give us her shopping list and money. Between the two of us, it was an easy task that we didn't mind doing together.

"Think she's ready for us?" Nathan asked as we neared the cottage.

"It's nearly noon. She's been awake for hours,"

I commented, rolling my eyes.

"Why do you hang out with her, Alex?" Nathan's voice had dropped, though he didn't sound accusatory.

I refused to look at him as I answered. "I learn from her. She's my best friend. And ... I love her, Nathan. She's the grandmother I never had. I love her."

"What do you learn from her?"

In all our years together, this was the first time he'd ever asked me anything. I had to wonder what the trigger was this time.

"Everything. Life. Herbs. Seasons. Knowledge of all kinds. Morgan teaches me whatever she can whenever she can."

"Does she teach you magic?"

I pressed on the brakes and allowed my bike to come to a stop. Beside me, Nathan did the same. It gave me the time I needed as I searched his face for any sign of what might have triggered his questions. In the four years we'd known each other, he had never demanded explanations from me. As part of our own code, he didn't ask questions he didn't want the answers to. If he was asking now, there had to be a reason.

My chin lifted a little and I kept a careful eye on his expression as I announced, "Yes, Nathan, she teaches me magick."

Nathan nodded once and pushed down on his bike pedal, continuing down Old Grove Road as if nothing had happened. For a moment, I could only stare after him. Then I shook my head and followed. Soon enough, we stood at the gate where Morgan awaited us. Her expression was a little distant, leading me to believe she somehow knew what had occurred. When she focused, however, a smile lit up her face and my own expression mirrored hers.

"Hello," I greeted her.

"Hello," Nathan said beside me. For once, he seemed almost relaxed in her presence. Yet, I could still sense the iron determination that was significant to him.

"Hello, my dears," Morgan responded. Her hands slipped from her shawl as she handed the shopping list and money to me.

"We'll be back soon," I promised her and she nodded.

"Take your time. *Do* try not to forget anything," Morgan added.

My gut clenched. Nathan and I had not forgotten a single thing on her list for the past four years. Why would I need a reminder now? *Something's going to happen today*, I thought yet again.

"We won't," I assured her in a tight voice. I was worried as well as suspicious. What did she know?

Sharing a last look, I turned my bike around and Nathan and I began pedaling toward town once more. Was it the reminder or the lullaby that had me even more on edge? I couldn't be sure. But you don't mess with signs. They had a tendency to predict more than you thought.

Like now.

We were just passing Wheelock Road when a car suddenly barreled out of the driveway I'd just passed. Nathan was a little behind me and had to swerve in place. I skidded to a stop as I whipped my bike around in time to see Nathan wipe out on the concrete. It was obvious that he had caught something. He was wearing shorts and his leg was scraped up. Nothing for a thirteen-year-old.

But for a thirteen-year-old's mom?

"Good thing my house isn't far from here,"

Nathan muttered as he stood his bike up. I cocked my head to the side and examined the wound as he put weight on it.

"It's not bad. Just wash it out and apply a little aloe to it and it'll be fine."

Nathan rolled his eyes. "You sound like my mom. My dad would just have me wash it out and pour peroxide on it."

I shrugged. "Either way, you have to wash it out. C'mon," I said with a resigned sigh.

I thought nothing of his falling. And whoever had pulled out of their driveway like that was a jerk. His wounds would heal quickly. Just a few scrapes. The whole situation was meaningless except for as a delay. At least, that's what I thought until we got to Nathan's house.

The two of us left our bikes in the driveway and walked in the front door. I was inching along since Nathan and I weren't normal friends and I'd never met anyone in his family other than his obnoxious brother. I stood in the hallway awkwardly as Nathan continued on toward the door at the end that I assumed was the bathroom.

Before he even reached it, a female voice called, "Nathan? Is that you? I didn't expect you back so soon."

My face drained of blood and my blue eyes grew wide. It couldn't be…

All too soon, a woman rounded the corner out of one of the other doorways and met up with Nathan. She was tall, with straight blond hair that gathered at her shoulders. Her nose was straight, her lips almost too thin to be attractive, with eyes that glittered a blue-green jade color. And she was absolutely familiar.

"Faylin!" I gasped.

The woman's blue eyes shot up to me and narrowed. Not in anger. Curiosity flared in them. In that instant, I knew that she was not the woman I had met at Morgan's, but the similarities were too numerous to ignore.

This was Faylin's twin sister.

"Who is your friend, Nathan?" his mother asked in a forced calm tone.

Nathan moved his surprised expression away from me and back to his mom. "Alex Ryder. She lives down on Verity Lane. You know…"

"The girl who found Alyssa Rice's body a few years back," I remarked in a dry tone. His mother's eyes never left mine and I just about refused to blink as I stared back. "I'm sorry. You look like someone I just met. A relative perhaps?"

Recognition caught in Nathan's features, from what I could see in my peripheral vision. "Oh! That might have been my Aunt Sarah. Mom and her are twins." It was the most personal piece of information Nathan had ever shared with me. And his mother hated it.

"Yep. I think that might have been it," I remarked. His mother looked away and I looked back at Nathan. "You should go clean up so we can get going," I told him.

"Yeah, alright," he replied rolling his eyes.

"Use aloe," his mother replied automatically and Nathan gave me a 'see, I told you' look.

As soon as Nathan left the room, his mom gestured me toward the kitchen. I followed her inside and it felt like the battle lines were about to be drawn. Would she give me the same useless warnings?

"I apologize for thinking you were Faylin."

"We do not use those names anymore. She is Sarah and I am Anne."

I felt my eyes widen. Why had she taken Anne's name? Did she even know who Anne was? Did she realize that they were not related? What *had* Morgan told them?

"Why do you allow your sons near her and Sarah freaks out over the possibility that her children can become involved with their own grandmother?" I demanded in a harsh whisper.

Anne's look was stern. "Do not use that title. Our children's grandmother is dead. Do you understand? I don't want Nathan to know about any of this," she hissed in a barely-audible whisper.

I had to take a deep breath before nodding. "I understand. It would confuse him if he ever found out."

Now Anne studied me. "You're more intuitive than Sarah let on. Of course, she was always a little on the rash side. Much like our own grandmother."

I wanted to shake my head. Faylin–Sarah–was nothing like how Victoria had been. But they knew of Alice, not Victoria. I had my answers, I guess.

"Fay and I didn't get along much. You and I, I hope, will be on better terms."

"And why should we be?" Anne asked skeptically.

"Because I want answers and you have them. Morgan tells me nothing of you because it is not her place. But it is yours. I would like to talk to you."

Anne was just about to shake her head no when Nathan walked into the room.

"Ready to go?" he asked me. I nodded, still not looking away from his mother.

Soon, I sent to her mind. Anne's eyes got wide. She nodded her head and I grinned as Nathan and I headed back out the front door.

"What was that about? You and my mom?" Nathan asked as soon as we were outside.

I shrugged. "Nothing. Just a few similarities."

Chapter Six

SHOPPING

How to confront Morgan about this? Because *obviously* I was going to confront her. Then I had to figure out what to say to Nathan's mom. What all did I want to know about the situation that she could tell me? Would I have to play detective again and use my psychometry to try and figure it out? How much would be shown to me this time? Did I want to see it all?

"Alex, you okay?" Nathan asked as we arrived at the market.

I shook my head slightly to come out of my daze. "Yeah. Just thinking. Now let's see..." Pulling the list from my pocket, I showed the needed items to Nathan.

"I'll start at this end and you start at the

other?"

"Isn't that how it's always done?" I asked with a sardonic smile.

Leaving our bikes, the two of us went inside and I made my way toward the toiletries while Nathan headed for canned goods. We would each bounce around in our areas of the store as we gathered what Morgan needed. For some reason, we never shopped together.

Today it was a particularly good thing. How could I keep such a huge secret from Nathan? Sure, we weren't *close*, but there was a weird honor code between us. To know something so big about him personally... There was nothing I could do. I had to keep my mouth shut.

"Hey. Thought that was you," a voice surprised me. I jumped and turned in the same instant.

Despite the smile that spread across my face at the sight of Matt, I was irritated with myself. My senses were dull. I was so lost in my thoughts that my natural defenses were slipping. I'd have to practice those later.

"Oh, hey," I greeted him, trying to act casual. "What're you doing here?"

"Shopping." He rolled his eyes. "My mom dragged me along."

"Let me guess, you get to haul all the heavy stuff?" I laughed.

Matt laughed and nodded. "Pretty much. So, what're you doing here?"

"Shopping for Morgan–my teacher." As evidence, I motioned to the basket of my half of the groceries.

"Is she a hermit, then?"

"Pretty much," I replied.

Matt nodded, unperturbed by my mention of Morgan. "So, after you're done shopping, what're you planning on doing?"

"Well, I'm going to be at Morgan's for a couple of hours. Then I'm heading down to the local watering hole."

"Cool. I'll probably see you there. I've got a little unpacking to do after this, but I should be down there about three o'clock."

I couldn't help my wide smile. "Sounds good. I'll see you around four, if you're still there."

"I'm pretty sure I will be," Matt replied. His wide smile made me feel less embarrassed by my own.

"Hey Alex, do you have everything yet?" Nathan's voice reached me as he rounded the corner with his own basket. He stopped dead when he saw me talking to Matt. For some odd reason, I had the faintest feeling like I should be blushing.

"Sorry. I got distracted," I told Nathan apologetically.

"No problem. Hey, Matt. How's it going?" Nathan asked him in a casual tone.

"Good. You?"

Okay, I guess they knew each other pretty well already. At the same time, it was like the conversation was too casual. Too polite. What was going on?

"Just fine. Alex, if you want, I can grab the rest of the stuff," Nathan added to me.

"No, it's fine. I've got it. Thanks anyway," I stated, a bit miffed at being kept out of the loop, and at the implication that just because a boy was present I couldn't do my job.

"Alright. I'll be near the registers when you're done. See ya later, man," he added to Matt.

"Yeah. See ya later." When Nathan had gone, Matt looked back at me. "Nathan shops for her, too?"

I began grabbing more items and adding them to the cart, determined to carry on the conversation and do my job at the same time. "Yeah. She pays him, though. I work on a volunteer basis," I said with a small, rueful chuckle.

"Cool. Well, uh, I gotta go. My mom's probably freaking out."

I nodded, already sure of what happened. Matt thought Nathan and I were a couple, and now he'd probably never talk to me again. Great.

"Yeah, sure. No problem. I know how moms can be," I stated in a polite voice.

Matt was already at the end of the aisle when he turned around. "You're still coming swimming later, right?"

And just like that, my mood was soaring. My smile lit up my whole face as I answered, "Yeah. Definitely."

Matt smiled back. "See ya then, Alex."

"See ya, Matt," I said just as he was disappearing around a corner.

Holding together my excitement, I hurriedly finished the shopping. I even double-checked everything to make sure there was nothing forgotten. Afterward, I headed up to the registers and Nathan transferred everything onto the counter. While I paid, he put away the baskets.

"Ready?" he asked, grabbing a handful of plastic bags.

"Yep," I answered as I gathered my handful.

I waved goodbye to the cashier and received the same tense expression I got every week. I was starting to earn the same fear from the town that Morgan had. I think that hurt me more than it had her, but maybe this was how she felt when it first began to happen to her.

The worst part was that I knew that I wouldn't have cared a couple of days ago. It would have been a normal event from the past four years. Just like everyone not talking to me. Just like the whispers that followed me out of the store. Just like the endless silence between Nathan and me. All of it was normal for me.

Because Matt talked to me, making me feel like less of an outsider yesterday, today I felt the sting that I hadn't felt four years ago. The painful prod of endless rejection and disappointment. I heard the fear behind those whispers now. And I knew with painful certainty that no one was ever going to accept me here.

I still wasn't running away.

Nathan and I rode our bikes back in companionable silence. When we reached Morgan's, he held the grocery bags while I parked my bike. Then I took all of the bags from him and entered the garden, carefully stepping over the salt line.

"Hello," I crooned to my Familiar. The black cat brushed my leg in greeting and I saw Nathan throw a small smile at her. I didn't know who was more surprised, me or the cat.

"See ya later, Alex," Nathan said as he turned his bike around.

"Going swimming later?" I surprised myself by asking.

"Yeah. You gonna make it again today?"

"I'm not allowed to hang out all day during the summer. Might as well go swimming," I replied with a shrug.

"See ya later, then."

"See ya."

I waited until Nathan left. I couldn't feel Morgan in the house, meaning she was out in the forest someplace. That left me to put the groceries away and await her return. As soon as Nathan was gone, another me appeared, taking half of the groceries from my hands.

Together, myself and I, walked into the small house and began putting away all of the groceries. A moment after my other self put away the last box of cereal, the sound of car tires pulling up in the seldom-used driveway piqued my interest.

Without even bothering to absorb my other self, we walked out the front door and looked over the flowers and plants to see a dark blue car sitting in the driveway. Morgan appeared in front of the car, her own astral self preceding her arrival.

It let me know that this was one of two people.

"Welcome home, Fiona," Morgan said as her daughter got out of the car.

"I didn't come here to speak with you, Mother. I'm here to talk to the girl."

Morgan nodded her head to me and Fiona-Anne-looked over the top of her car at me. She blinked once, then again. When she realized that the other person was really my projection, her eyes widened in appreciation.

"She's powerful," she seemed to murmur to herself.

"More powerful than my own daughters. She set the circle with her Wiccaning."

Fiona's mouth dropped open and she stared at her mother in utter shock. "Impossible. The Coven's tried for centuries to set the circle. They've never even come close. No amount of good poured into that place could set it after Mary's burning."

"What do you know about it?" I asked, taking a step forward. "What do you know about Mary Sullivan?"

"Not as much as I wish I did. The same as you, obviously," Anne remarked.

"Should we go for a walk?" I suggested.

"Let's go."

Chapter Seven

TRADE

"First thing's first: you promise me you'll never tell my sons anything I say. I don't want Tyler or Nathan knowing anything about this. As far as they are concerned, my parents are dead. Sarah's the only family they know of. I don't plan on changing that and I won't have you telling them, either. Do you understand me?"

Jeez! Another fricken mom look. Would they never learn?

"I can't promise that. I don't make promises. Not to anyone. But I can tell you I will keep it to myself for as long as possible.

Anne gave me a studying look. "You won't promise?"

"No, I won't. However, I do know how to keep

things to myself. And I'm going to get my answers either way, so you might as well tell me."

"Well, if you won't promise, at least give me a trade. I will tell you about growing up under the care of your teacher, and you will tell me about you and your life here under her guardianship."

"I can do that, I guess."

"I'll start, then. What do you want to know?"

"Your sister mentioned a promise Morgan made to you. About not teaching another who did not wish to learn. Morgan forced you?" I asked, my voice layered with skepticism.

"It was not to me whom she made that vow to. It was to our elder sister. She was named Freyja by our mother. She's two years older than Sarah and I. She moved away the day that Sarah and I turned eighteen. It was to her my mother made that promise."

I had to take a minute to absorb that. "Three daughters. Freyja, Fiona, and Faylin. All of you had bad experiences with magick, causing you to pull away. Your twin fights against it. Freyja disappeared, avoiding it. And you... You use the practical parts of what you were taught, but you buried your magick deep inside."

"You do see clearly, don't you?"

I shrugged. "In magick, you have to learn to see clearly. Clouded vision leads to bad results. Which is what caused Faylin's disastrous experiences."

"How do you know that?" Anne asked in a patronizing and amused tone.

"I don't need to be psychometric to see that one. Though I probably will sooner or later. With what she implied, she played with fire and got burned. I'm almost certain that the Threefold Law kicked her ass."

That was assuming she followed the Wiccan Threefold Law. Not many solitary witches did, but it was a good rule for young witches to follow if they had a lot of power and too many reasons to use it. If a witch believed in something with enough faith, it would begin to shape their reality. I knew that the Threefold Law shaped parts of mine, despite the fact that I was nowhere close to Wiccan.

Anne shook her head at my language. "You are right. She cast a love spell when she was fifteen. We'd just started high school and her spell didn't specify what kind of love. She drew it to her, but her boyfriend turned out to be…"

"A dick?" I offered expertly.

Anne's look was rueful. "Yes. That. It hurt Sarah, and she never forgave our mother for teaching us to use the Craft. I think that was the primary reason our eldest sister made the deal with our mother. Of course, the irony was that they were just alike, our mother and sister. Exactly alike.

"Anyway, I had a similar bad experience with magick. I thought my spell would protect someone I love from making bad choices. It didn't. After accepting the fact that the Craft couldn't make life easier, I stopped using. It's like a drug, Alex. You use and use and use and before you know it, you've used too much and the addiction starts to set in. So here is my advice: stop. And if you don't, at least use it sparingly."

"But there's a difference between you and me," I began to argue and she cut me off.

"That is what everyone thinks, but it's not about the users being different. The substance never changes. Everything lies in a balance. Including the mundane and the magickal. You can't go through a whole life of using magick and not expect to pay the balance for it. Not even the most powerful witch in the world could escape paying the price of it.

"We daughters of Morgan learned the hard way. Because of that, we each have let magick drift out of our lives. No matter how powerful we are, we don't use it."

A lengthy silence fell between us, until I was forced to admit, "I don't know what else to say."

"What else do you want me to tell you?"

"Everything," I answered, my curiosity raging.

"Very well," Anne sighed. Then she launched into a life story, answering many of the questions I had.

The bedroom was added after the twins were born. It was used for the three daughters whilst Morgan slept in the main room. All of which occurred after their father suffered a work re-lated accident and died from his injuries. The twins both shaped the gargoyles out of stone, as all three daughters had inherited an amazing gift of shaping stone. As it turned out, it was Freyja who had shaped my face into the bench her mother had made. A thought that made me realize that I was at the maiden stage of life. Our faces matching up identically.

As the story continued, I realized how hard it must have been growing up in the tiny house with all those females. I also realized how different it must have been growing up with magick from their very first breaths. It was no wonder they all tanked in experiences with it. They didn't respect it. They didn't know how to, growing up with it so young. I, at least, knew what respect was from the moment I learned to talk. Magick came later for me. And that was what had messed up Morgan's daughters.

Lack of respect. No self-discipline. Petty. Selfish. Emotional. And that was just Faylin.

Hesitant. Lack of confidence. Faithless. Fearful. That was Fiona.

Too much like her mother; stubborn, always right, willful, domineering. Incredibly powerful. Freyja was a carbon copy of her mother. She saw what the magick was doing to the twins and she put the collar on her mother before the same could happen to anyone else. Freyja did it to protect others; not because magick was bad, but because some people just weren't meant to know how to use it. Not once was it mentioned–or known–if Freyja continued to practice herself or not. She didn't keep in contact.

At last, Anne stopped talking, having explained everything I wanted to know. That I could think of right now.

"Alright. Now it's your turn. What happened four years ago?"

I sighed. "Remember that you asked. If you don't believe me, that is your choice."

Anne nodded at my warning before urging me to continue.

So I told her. I described my first encounters with Alyssa. My suspicions on her location. Finding a way into the attic. And how Alyssa helped to set off my powers. Then I told her about my Wiccaning and the powerful aftereffects. I finished with the story with Alyssa's death and Victoria's justice.

Anne was stunned.

By the time I had finished, we had come full circle and were standing out by her car once more. Glancing at the sundial, I realized we'd been talking for hours, Anne and I. But it was for the best that we learn these things about one another.

"Take a day before you decide whether you believe me or not," I suggested as we paused.

Anne nodded. "I will have to. And I hope you will take what I said under advisement," she hinted and I nodded in return. "Then this is goodbye. Until I see you again, Alex."

"Goodbye," I replied and she opened the car door.

Before getting in the vehicle, Anne looked back at me with an almost worried expression. "Alex? Just how close are you and Nathan?"

I smiled a little at that. "His voice is barely familiar to me. Does that answer your question?"

Her smile was a little strange. "It does. Thank you."

"You're welcome. I will see you some other time."

With our last goodbyes out, Anne soon left her mother's property. Now was the time to discuss this all with Morgan. If she would even talk to me about it.

Chapter Eight

INTRODUCTION

"You have questions. You always have questions," Morgan mused as I came into the little house where she was preparing food for the two of us.

"I do."

As much as I loved Morgan, there was always that layer of respect that kept her from being more than a teacher at certain times. Whenever I was spending the night, however, it seemed as though she was my grandmother. Our relationship was strange.

"Why did you force them? You never seemed the type to force magick," I asked quietly.

"I forced them because I didn't want them to miss out on what Freyja and I had. She was so powerful. So full of promise. It was because of her that I had expected even more from the twins. I shouldn't have. Faylin was the youngest and most envious of Freyja's powers. She wanted so much to be like her sister that she was willing to do anything to call power to her. That should have been my first warning that magick would not mesh well with that child. Fiona was always so timid in her approach to it, but she was the best herbal witch I've ever come across to this day. She gathered all of nature's knowledge and improved lives with it. I do wish she had gone to medical school as she had planned. Alas, she got pregnant and married her high school sweetheart. She was the only one whom love could find in this town."

"What about Faylin? She hates magick so much now."

"Oh no, Alexandria, Faylin could never hate magick. She hates me for teaching it to her. Yet, she hates me more for her not having more power. She envied Freyja her magick. The reason she is so against it now is because she was bitten by it, and it was proven that she should have never learned."

"And Freyja? What happened to her?" A wave of sadness hit me right then and I was consumed with everlasting grief.

"Freyja died the day the twins turned eighteen."

My mouth fell open and my eyes grew wide. Everything in me screamed 'impossible' but the despair filling up the small house told me it was true.

"How?" I gasped.

"I don't know. She was always so secretive. Come the day Fiona and Faylin aged eighteen, Freyja walked away. She disappeared. Later that night, I felt it. When you have a child, you will know what I mean. They become a part of you. Freyja was so much a part of me that when she died, it almost killed me, too."

"Fiona and Faylin never knew," I whispered, the distinction becoming clear.

"No. Freyja never wanted any of us to know. I am sure of that. I am also sure that she knew she was going to die. She chose to see her sisters to the age of majority before deciding that it was time to leave us for good."

"If you didn't tell them, why are you telling

me?" I whispered.

"Because you asked, and you won't be pained by her absence."

"Well, there is where you're wrong. You should know by now that anything that pains you pains me. Maybe not as much, but it does. And seeing as how this summer is playing out already, I won't be surprised if I end up meeting Freyja. You know how seldom spirits leave me be once I've learned even one thing about them."

"No." Morgan shook her head in denial but we both knew that I was probably right. Twice more, I'd been called upon to help aid spirits once I became aware of them. Alyssa was the first. She would never be the last.

"For both our sakes, I hope that is not the case. However, I think I'm going to be facing more this year than I have done in years past. I am thirteen, now, and I will Ascend this year," I murmured.

Morgan's eyes shot to my face, piercing into me with that icy gaze. "You're sure?"

I nodded. "The visions only become clearer over time. You and I will be at the circle and I will Ascend. My powers now are nothing compared to what they will be then."

My voice was subdued as I thought about that. I barely knew what to do with my magick at the strength it was at now. What was going to happen then?

Before anything else could be said, my inner clock tipped me off as to the time. Looking at the clock on the mantel, I saw that it was fifteen minutes to four. My time was up. Everything else could wait until later.

"Go. Enjoy the life you have," Morgan murmured as she noticed my distraction.

I smiled at her. "Thank you. And ... I'm sorry about Freyja. I'm sorry for how her death affected you."

"As am I," she whispered.

Without thinking about it, I threw my arms around her. I let my emotions flow from me to her without a single block. My love, my sorrow, my pity, and my caring. All of it flowed from me to her and I could feel all of it returned. For whatever reason, she felt all the same things for me.

"You know, Lex, sometimes I muse that Freyja led you to me. Just so I could have a companion once more. A young person I would learn to respect and love once more."

"You know what, Morgan? I think she did, too."

After another long minute, I let go and disappeared out the door. As I walked down the path, I found my beautiful, jade-eyed, nameless Familiar following me. I pet her, fully expecting her to turn around and disappear back into the house or garden. She didn't. Even when I pulled my bike from its resting place on the fence, she was right there.

"You want to meet him?" I guessed, staring at her clever jade eyes.

In an instant, she perked up.

"Want a ride?" I asked with a devious grin, indicating the basket on the front of my bike. The thing was an antique and the basket was wire, but I kept a jacket in it for instances like this.

In answer, my Familiar wrapped around my legs in a figure eight. Laughing, I reached down and picked her up. Taking liberties, I kissed her once on her furry head before placing her gently into the basket. Were she not used to this, she might have been a little leerier about the ride.

Climbing astride the bike, I pushed off and began pedaling toward the end of Old Grove Road where a lake sat that was perfect for swimming. It was not a long ride and I found myself there sooner than I expected. My Familiar looked over the top of the basket as I pulled the bike to the side of the road and parked it along with the others.

Letting my Familiar leave the basket, I did what I was always forced to do. Ever since I was nine, my bike was targeted for mischief. After a few slashed tires, I grew sick of it and conjured up a protection spell. Now, should anyone think of harming it, their thoughts would get sidetracked and they would leave it be.

"Let's go," I said to my feline friend once my work was complete.

With the cat trailing me, I headed toward the water. While I walked, I pulled the ponytail from my wrist and pulled my hair back. As I reached the water's edge, I carefully did not look around for Matt. My Familiar, however, had no such scruples.

"Hey there," I heard his voice coo. I smiled to

myself as I had sensed him from the moment we had arrived, setting my instincts back on track.

Glancing over, I watched as Matt crouched down to pet my friend. The jade-eyed critter stopped two feet away. Sitting down, her furry head cocked to the side a few times as she studied him. I waited to see whether or not she would hiss or claw at him, or if she'd let him approach her.

Instead of doing anything, the cat lifted a paw and began to lick it. That was a surprise. I'd seen her hostile. I'd seen her accepting and nice. Never apathetic. Matt inched a little closer, but the cat gave him one of her signature looks and he stopped. She honestly didn't care.

So, what did that mean for me? Trust him? Or not?

"Matt! Dude, leave the cat alone," one of his buddies commented in a forced casual tone.

My expression turned sardonic. "Yeah. She'd walk up to you if she liked you. And all the kids here are afraid of black cats. We have reputations."

Matt grinned before glancing back to see all the scowls the others were giving me. Shaking his head, Matt chuckled.

"Superstitious?" Matt remarked.

"They have a right to be. She chose me."

"And if she doesn't like me?"

"I wouldn't talk to you anymore. Lucky for you, she can't seem to decide whether or not you're worth her time. I think that means we can continue talking until she makes up her mind about you." My smile was sly.

"Because of a cat, you'd stop talking to me?"

"Does she look like a normal cat to you?"

Matt made a show of studying my Familiar for another few seconds. "Nope." His lips popped on the 'p' and caused me to laugh.

"Exactly. So, did you come with the peanut gallery, or are they just that paranoid?" I questioned, pointing my chin in direction of the other kids.

Matt glanced over his shoulder as they all turned away. Rolling his eyes, Matt commented, "Paranoid."

"Well, I guess I'll leave you alone then. Don't want them to have premature heart attacks," I replied. My smile was a little rueful. Since we had run out of conversation, however, I couldn't find a reason to impose myself on him any longer.

"What if I don't want you to leave me alone?" Matt asked as I made to walk away.

Surprised, I turned back to face him. The smile on my face could not get larger.

"Then I guess I won't. If you're sure…"

"I'm sure." The crinkle-eyed smile he gave me was a deciding factor.

"Then I won't."

A moment of silence lasted between us until the cat gave a tired meow before she turned to head back toward home. I could have sworn she was walking away because our sad attempts at flirting were disgusting her. Her black tail flicked through the air as she disappeared into the brush. I laughed at the display before meeting Matt's eyes once more.

"We going swimming or what?"

"Definitely," Matt answered.

He removed his shirt at the water's edge and I found myself stealing glances at him. His chest and stomach showed the beginning definition of someone who either played a lot of sports or worked out in their free time. It wouldn't have surprised me to learn that it was both. With the muscle definition in his arms, it was almost impossible to say that he didn't lift weights at some point. Though he had the build of a runner. Easy football player status right there.

For a minute, I allowed myself to study him. Part of me thought I should start blushing at some point, because if anyone noticed it'd be embarrassing. At the same time, I felt zero shame in checking him out. As far as I was concerned, there was no harm in admiring something I found attractive. If guys could do it to girls, I would be happy to reciprocate.

"Alex? You coming?" Matt asked, snapping me from my reverie.

"Yeah," I replied, slipping out of my shorts and pulling my shirt over my head. I had one foot in the water when it hit me. With a gasp, the images flew through my mind.

Victoria's dress drifted out behind her as she strode into the cold water. The voices of the Coven drifted over the lake's surface as they called on the water to take her to her grave, and keep her forever at the bottom of the lake. Inky black tendrils of hair drifted across the surface until her face disappeared into the magical chasm.

Then the scene abruptly shifted.

Standing up to her knees in the lake was a young woman of no more than twenty years. The same inky black hair hung below her waist and the dress she wore was a replica of the ceremonial robes Victoria had last worn. Icy blue eyes bored into mine as the girl looked over her frail shoulder. Just as the young woman turned back toward the cold water, the vision disappeared.

Freyja. I had no doubt.

"Cold, isn't it?" Matt chuckled. The world was brought back into focus as I stared at his gloating face. He was teasing me as the goosebumps appeared over most of the exposed skin on my body.

"Yeah. Cold."

Chapter Nine

DATE

I wasn't the only one surprised by how much time Matt spent with me. Even after we were done swimming that day, we sat by the side of the lake and talked for a long time. He regaled me with tales from California whilst I informed him of the small town he had just moved to. When our time was up and I was getting ready to go, he asked if I'd be coming back tomorrow. I smiled and told him I would and he seemed pleased.

The next day, the pattern repeated. Then again the following day. Again. And again. Suddenly, two weeks had passed and I found that we had done the same thing every single day. Instead of getting bored with the stability, I was actually quite content with it.

Then things changed.

"Hey, Alex," Matt accosted me as I was heading for my bike.

Laughing, I turned and said, "Matt, I've been here every day for the past two weeks. I'll be here tomorrow."

Matt closed his mouth, looking slightly embarrassed or shy. "That's not what I was going to ask."

"Wasn't it?" I challenged, not buying that for a second.

"No, it wasn't," Matt replied, a tiny grin teasing at the corners of his mouth. His tone was just as challenging as mine and I perked up at the idea of one of our fun arguments. We'd had a few already in the past couple of days and our debates were always enjoyable.

"Alright then: surprise me. What were you going to ask that was not the same as every day for the past fourteen days?"

"Would you like to go out with me tomorrow night?" The words were blunt and so casually spoken-without a hint of hesitation-that I almost laughed at them. Almost.

After looking at him in shock for a minute,

I managed, "You're serious?"

"Do I look like I'm kidding?" Again, so casual as to almost make you think he was joking.

"No, but I'm still not sure what to say," I murmured.

A crooked grin alighted on his face as he looked at me. "Say yes."

I began shaking my head. "I'd have to ask my parents. I'm not allowed to date until I'm fifteen. I doubt my dad will say it's okay."

Matt shrugged. "So, don't tell them."

The idea was tempting, but the idea of lying to my parents didn't sit well with me. Of course, if I could talk my way into spending the night at Morgan's, it was a conceivable option. All it would take was one little half-truth.

"Alright. It's a date," I replied with a small smile.

I watched with pleasure as Matt's eyes lit up. "If you're not telling your parents, then I guess I will meet you...?"

"Up town by the movie theater, if you want?"

"Sounds great. I'll see you tomorrow," Matt replied as he went to walk past me.

I watched him as he got on his bike and rode

away, my heart feeling light while butterflies burst through my stomach. I was going on my first date. Nerves traveled all through my body and I couldn't stop smiling as I pondered that fact.

Now all I had to do was convince Morgan to let me spend the night with her and then tell my parents about it. Yeah, that just added to the nerves.

Instead of going straight home, I headed to Morgan's.

Can I spend the night? I felt that sending the message ahead of myself might prepare Morgan more before she saw my face. Which would make her suspicious.

"What is the reason?" Morgan asked as I walked through the door. She never encouraged my reading thoughts. Sending messages: okay. Listening to drifting thoughts: invasion of privacy.

"It's silly and frivolous and really, *really* important to me," I began in a pleading tone. Morgan raised a single feathery brow at me and I sighed. "Matt asked me out on a date and I said yes."

"Go home, Lex." She didn't even pause to think about it and her immediate answer made my mouth drop.

"But ... my parents!"

"Your mother will be thrilled. Trust me. And she will see to it that your father comes around. I'll not tell you again, Alexandria. Go home."

For a long time, I just stood there. My mouth was still open. My eyes were still wide in surprise. And a feeling of dejection and betrayal twisted in my stomach.

But what choice did I have? Morgan was not going to help me. That left me to trust in my mother's indulgence. Something that was more reliable four years ago.

Without saying or thinking a word to my mentor, I turned on my heel and strode out of the tiny cottage, down the stone path, through the gate and over the salt line, to my bicycle. My mind was churning the whole way home. What would I say to my parents?

By the time I got home, I was thoroughly worked up. It wasn't in my nature to admit defeat by any means. And if I was the master of half-truths, I was also the ingenious manipulator of my mother. Who knew? Maybe she'd get a kick out of my first date. I knew my dad wouldn't but if anyone could persuade him, my mother could. Not that they could stop me, even if they said no. I was going with or without their permission.

"Hey, honey."

I blinked in surprise at my mother's greeting. Being so used to the everyday movements, I'd made it home, put my bike up, and even walked through the kitchen door all without really realizing where I was. Odd. *I really need to keep a better focus on my surroundings.*

"Oh, hey Mom."

"Something wrong?" My mother's brows pulled together in concern as she studied me with the same face I was rapidly achieving. Identical blue eyes trailed over my body, making sure there was nothing out of place that would be reason for alarm. Those same lips puckered as she took in my wet hair and bright eyes.

"Nothing's wrong, Mom," I commented in a hesitating tone. This was on purpose. If I'd said an adamant 'nothing's wrong' then she would ponder over it more, but she wouldn't ask any questions. Right now, I needed her to question.

"Then what's up?" Her eyes sharpened though her tone remained casual.

"Is Dad home?" Again, I made my voice reluctant.

"Not at this time. Why?"

I took a deep breath and let it whoosh out of my mouth as though something was weighing heavily on my shoulders. In truth, it wasn't. I was going on this date either way, but it would be nice if I didn't have to split myself in two for my first real date.

"Lex, tell me what's going on," my mother demanded in a warning tone.

"It's nothing bad, Mom," I remarked with a flicker of a smile on my face. This allowed her to relax a little bit. "It's just... I... You know what, just forget it. I'll be in my room."

I'd taken exactly three steps before my mother intercepted me.

"You're not getting out of this that easily. What did you want to tell me?"

"Nothing," I insisted in the voice of a whiny teenager.

"Alexandria Marie Ryder."

"Fine!" I sighed dramatically, choosing to

sit on one of the stools at the island. "It's about Matt."

"And you didn't want to talk about this? Things getting serious?" my mother replied in a joking tone.

I looked up at her through my lashes in a guilty expression. "He asked me out on a date." My voice barely came out in a whisper, along with some genuine excitement.

Now my mom sat down on a stool beside me and her face was set into an expression of shock. I didn't understand why until she whispered, "My baby's all grown up."

There were a number of ways I could take that. Deciding which one would increase my chances of success, however, was a bit difficult.

"Not grown up enough. I told Matt that I wasn't allowed to date yet."

My mother's blue eyes widened in surprise at my forlorn tone. Keeping my eyes on my lap in a sad expression, I waited.

"Call Matt. Schedule the date. I'll deal with your father."

Of course, the following was expected. I jumped up in excitement and fawned gratefully over my mother for a good five minutes before taking the phone up to my room. I really did call Matt in order to let him know that my mom had given me the go-ahead. Afterward, Mom and I spent an hour in the kitchen gushing over various details of boys and dating in general. She gave me *lots* of advice. Not sure how much of it was pertinent to me, but whatever.

I had a cute, sapphire dress on that made me appear grown and mature. My brunette hair was curled and held back with a black hair piece. There was even a light layer of makeup on my face. Something that had almost made my father ban the date altogether. I half wondered if the reason he didn't was because he knew that I was just like him, and would go even if they told me not to.

Waiting outside the theater, I was growing nervous. And a bit paranoid. Was this a set-up? See how desperate the witch-girl was for a date? How long would she wait around before she realized Matt was a no-show? Just before I was about to give up, a blue Dodge sedan pulled up and Matt got out of the passenger seat.

"Sorry I'm late. We didn't miss the movie, did we?" he asked apologetically, looking behind me where the crowd was disappearing.

"You're forgiven. Just because we didn't miss it," I replied, trying to act more normal since I was so nervous I was almost shaking.

As we moved toward the ticket booth, an odd feeling came over me. Almost as if I were being watched. Turning in place I found the source. My jade-eyed Familiar stared after me. It was as if she were telling me to be careful. Nodding my head to her, I turned back to Matt as he paid for our tickets.

I understood the warning more after we entered the theater. There were a number of kids we knew there, ready to watch the latest romantic comedy. No big deal, I would have thought. Then they all did double-takes when they saw me walk in with Matt. After all, I had only been to the theater a few times, and never with a boy. In my already nervous state, this was not something I had anticipated or wished to put up with.

Then Matt grabbed my hand and I felt a surge of energy shoot through me. Smiling at him, I let him lead me down to the middle rows and we were able to sit in the aisle seats undisturbed. Even after we sat down, Matt didn't let go of my hand and it sent a rush of pleasure through me.

The lights had just dimmed and Matt and I were nice and comfortable in our seats. As the opening trailers were wrapping up, someone shouted, "Witch!" In the same instant, I sensed something being thrown at me. There was no time to react as I turned toward the missile.

It hit an invisible wall maybe six inches from my face. The half-full cup splashed against the shield before dropping to the floor. As one, the entire theater gasped. Feeling stunned, I turned slowly in my seat to look at Matt. He would know now. And he'd never want to talk to me again.

Matt was staring at me with wide, shocked eyes. I couldn't look at his face. With tears welling up in my eyes, I stood up and turned away from him. Before I could take another step, Matt grabbed my hand. Feeling yet more surprise, I turned back to look at him. He smiled at me.

"Let's just watch the movie," he suggested in a calm, casual tone. As if he hadn't seen me perform magick right then.

Too bewildered to say anything, I sat back down. Together, Matt and I continued to watch the movie. The whole time, he did not let go of my hand.

Chapter Ten

MAGICK AT MIDNIGHT

I was beyond excited when I got home. My mom was laughing with me as we drove and I told her about all the safe stuff that happened. I told her about people staring at me and how Matt just took my hand. She thought that was sweet.

As we got home, I barely said hi to my dad, leaving my mom to fill him in, before I bounded up to my room. Throwing my coat down on the bed, I felt myself spinning and spinning around in my room. I was so full of wonder that my magick took me to uncontrolled extremes. Before I knew it, my head was brushing the ceiling as I contin-ued to spin. Laughing, I eased myself back to the floorboards.

I was reckless with my magick that night.

After touching down on the floor, I went to take a shower before cleaning up my room a bit. I was just waiting for my parents to go to bed. At least, that's what I intended.

The movie had ended at nine, leaving me hours of anxious boredom. I'd paced my room so much I was surprised there wasn't a track worn into the floor, and I couldn't count how many times I lit the fire before extinguishing it.

At eleven, I couldn't wait anymore. Changing into my long, black ceremonial robes and witch's hat, I grabbed my besom-a broom I made back when I was nine-and went to my window. Opening the casement, I turned back only to let loose my astral self. After standing a moment in the center of the room, dressed in pajamas, I watched myself turn and climb into bed. Smiling, I turned back and leapt out the window.

Of course, I felt more and more like a stereotypical witch as I rode away on a broomstick. Cliché was definitely the word as I soared through the sky. Gaining in height, I even cackled as I watched Cedar Creek pass by below me.

I think I flew for about an hour. Then I made a snap-decision that I would never have made without consulting Morgan. I went to the circle. I was going to do a prosperity spell. After all, I was in such a good mood that others should be too.

Landing in the center of the circle, I could feel the power flux around me. It filled me and my own natural power seemed to increase ten-fold. This circle and I had a history. A rough one, on my part. During my Wiccaning-a ceremony similar to a baptism-I had entered into another woman's body as she was being burned alive. An act that had polluted the circle beyond salvation for hundreds of years. Then my Wiccaning had purified it, setting the balance straight. We were part of each other now.

I didn't need supplies as I stood there. The power coursing through me was enough. When I closed my eyes, I could hear the earth singing. Resonating voices called out to me, asking me to add my voice. So, I did. My intent was simple, to cast good will, health, and prosperity on those who deserved it. All around me, the magick spread, fading into the forest and going to cloak itself around all those in the little town of Cedar Creek and maybe even beyond.

After such a burst of magick, I guess I should have expected what happened next.

Morgan burst through the trees, her expression furious. At once, the magick seemed to die down, becoming a low hum in my blood instead of a forceful flood.

"Alexandria Ryder! What have you done?"

I felt chagrinned and let go of all magick except for what it took to keep my astral self in bed miles away from me. Taking my besom, I took slow, measured steps toward her while allowing my face to express my sorrow at making her upset.

"Did ... did I do it wrong?" I whispered. The thought of unleashing something unknown, instead of the prosperity I intended was stomach-clenching.

"What were you trying to do?" Her voice was as cold as ice, causing me to flinch.

"A prosperity spell. Good things. I only meant to send good things." I instantly reminded myself of being nine years old and just starting out, instead of a girl who would Ascend this summer.

Morgan sighed and I felt a little bit better. "That you did. But you sent out a lot, Lex. Remember, sending out too much good could alter the balance. We can't afford to have it altered."

"The circle didn't even absorb it," I argued. My good hadn't touched the circle, though I hadn't thought about that prior to my spell.

"Not the circle, Lex. The world. Too much good affects the world as does too much bad. A balance is preferable."

"My Ascension … will that sway the circle?" I demanded, a whisper of a warning gliding down my spine.

"No. An Ascension is as a birth or death: neutral." There was a long silence. "Your Ascension will happen this summer." Not a question.

"Yes."

"Good."

I wondered about that. Was she just that eager to have me Ascend to get to work on the real training? Did she think me capable of handling things after my Ascension without her? What was she planning?

The rest of the walk to her cottage was done in silence. I still wasn't sure how she felt about my midnight flight. She'd probably be upset. But I was just having a little fun.

We walked silently into the house where Morgan swept past me toward the kitchen portion of the main room. With her back to me she asked, "Your besom is with you because?"

"It's kind-of how I got here..."

There was a long silence before I heard a low chuckle. "I did the same thing when I was your age. Right after I made a besom big enough. I waited until Samhain night. My mother was so irate," Morgan chuckled.

I laughed with her. Setting my besom by the front door, I hung my hat on it. Then I sat down in my normal spot and waited for Morgan. That's when I noticed the tea sitting on the coffee table and I reached for it.

All of a sudden, the entire tray was wrenched away from me and sitting on top of the counter. I stared after it in surprise. Even I couldn't make objects move that smoothly or that quickly without a noise.

"That tea is not something for you to be drinking, Alexandria."

"Um. Okay," I said in a slow, confused tone.

"It is best to trust me on this, Lex."

"I do," I told her. Maybe there was some herb

in there that helped her with her joints or something. I understood that.

"I'm glad. Now, why don't we have some hot chocolate and cookies before I send you on your way?" The look she gave me was amused and I grinned.

"Sounds good to me."

With magick, always honing our skills, we made the hot chocolate and ate some of the cookies she had made earlier. Magickal baking was always the best. After our early morning snack, it was time for me to go.

As I reached the door, Morgan said my name, causing me to turn. She was standing by the fireplace, her back to me. There was a small chest on the mantel that had always sat there but had never been opened in my presence. It was open now. Morgan held something in her hands that she could only stare at.

"Come here, Lex." The words were a whisper and I walked slowly to where she stood. When she turned, her hands hid the object from view. "Hold out your hand."

I did as she asked without looking at my hands, keeping my eyes on hers. Then I felt the weight of a necklace fall into my hand. The chain sifted through my fingers and a solid round mass rested in my open palm.

Endless minutes passed as we watched each other. At last, Morgan glanced toward my hand and my blue eyes followed hers. A silver locket was settled against the skin, radiating a small amount of heat that came from magick it had absorbed over the years. The aura of magick embracing the small piece of jewelry was so potent, it was almost visible to the untrained eye.

Holding half a breath, I opened the tiny clasp. Though it looked every bit a normal locket, there were no pictures inside of it. Instead, there was a tiny clock. Morgan's magick coursed through it, constantly turning the gears that kept it going. Each little tick was a reminder of how much magick was stored in time itself. And how much time it took to learn magick.

"It's beautiful," I whispered to my mentor.

Morgan smiled and lifted it from my hand. Taking the chain, she walked behind me and fastened the locket around my neck. "It's yours."

As it settled against my neck, my psychometry sparked.

I closed the necklace behind my head before sweeping my hand beneath my black hair to have it flow over the silver chain. My mother had given it to me as a birthday present. A Samhain gift, as it were. It had belonged to her real mother, Victoria. The one I was almost identical to.

The magick pulsing through it soothed me. Like a lullaby. It would help me hide it better. My pain. My anger. My sense of being a leader with no followers. My knowledge of having no place in the world where I fit, because I was a much older soul with only new souls surrounding me. No one understood.

You die without a meaning in life. You waste away. Drown in your own unfulfilled desires. Decay in your skin because you have no use for it.

That's what I was doing. Dying without reason every single day. My breath became shallower each day. My heart beat less with each hour. Despite all the magick in my blood, even it was slipping away.

You die without a purpose.

I was dying.

I dragged in a ragged breath as my eyes filled

with tears. I met Morgan's eyes with my own and knew that I would never, ever tell her the truth. Freyja hadn't been sick. She'd just been wasting away. While her magick had given her power, it had not given her a purpose. She had died because of it.

Chapter Eleven

PRIDEFUL SOUL

Instead of riding my besom home, I decided to take the trail through the woods. I needed time to think before I would have to face another day. A long walk home at night meant there was no better time. After setting protection spells on me, I disappeared into the night.

Knowledge burst through my veins as I pondered each and every second that I had spent in the past as Freyja. It was different with her than it was being Alyssa or Victoria. This woman I had a chance of knowing. This woman I seemed to take after. Yet, this woman had died of a broken spirit.

Deep down I knew that feeling she had had. The want to do something great with your life. The desire to help shape the world into a better place.

The absolute need to lead others down the right path and to change lives in impossible ways. In short: to leave our mark on the world.

I was just young enough not to give up hope that I might one day do that.

Freyja had reached twenty-one and had known that her chance would never come. It was probably about my age that she began to realize that her life was without purpose. Her one hope was derived from the past; from a time when valor, honor, integrity, pride, dignity, respect, honesty, loyalty, and trustworthiness still meant—not something—*everything*. Basically, the soul inhabiting Freyja's body had slipped in from the Arthurian age.

A soul similar to hers was inside of me, I knew. But my soul had more hope or, perhaps, just more pride than hers. I would not—could not—admit defeat. It was impossible for me to say that, no matter how terrible this world was, I was incapable of changing anything; incapable of leaving my mark. That was something I could not accept by any means.

It was as I was drifting through the forest that my mind was made to focus on my astral self. Someone was coming into my room, I could feel it. I left my astral alone, allowing her to remain 'sleeping' and instead used remote viewing to watch my father ease into the room. Quiet as could be, he came and sat on my bed, watching my supposed sleeping form.

That was too much for me. Throwing my leg over my besom, I allowed my body and besom to change like a chameleon. We blended into the atmosphere and disappeared into our surroundings. Then I lifted off and sped home as fast as my besom allowed.

I don't know what I planned on once I got there. It wasn't like I could just barge into my own room with my father right there. I was invisible, not intangible. The chances of me getting in unnoticed were slim-to-nil. Then again, if the windows mysteriously burst open and I was able to slip inside...

There wasn't any time to second guess myself. Raising up to the height of the window, I waited for the perfect moment before using my ability to throw the casements wide open. Without hesitation, I zoomed through and opened my closet door. While my dad rushed to the window to close it, I put my besom away and closed the door silently before hiding in a corner out of his way.

The Marine glared out the window for several seconds before closing the casements and pulling the curtains into place. I didn't understand why he was here. And so late, too. My dad was one of those people that could lay his head down and was out like a light. I watched him closely as he moved back to the bed.

I smiled as he took the exact same route. He had counted his footsteps and knew where to stop and move aside in order to avoid objects in my room. At last, he made to sit on the end of my bed. That was when things got weird.

"Oh, Lexi Girl," he sighed quietly so as not to wake me. "I couldn't sleep tonight. I'm sure you don't even need a guess to know why. You were always so smart. Got that from your mom. Two smartest women I was ever blessed to have in my life. Sometimes I wonder if you're too smart for your own good."

I swallowed a little bit at that. This was starting to have some strange connotations. Of course, he was right about the clever thing, but still. Where was he going with this?

"I wonder if I did the right thing. Keeping us here, I mean. How can you ever find peace in this town with what happened to you? Your mom told me how you felt about everyone treating you like a freak. I'm so sorry baby. If I'd known, we would have left as soon as... We'd have been gone a long time ago."

This was worse than I thought. Was he trying to talk himself into moving? Moving my mom? Me? From Cedar Creek? From Morgan? I just about had a panic attack. If I didn't have a charade to keep up, my doppelgänger would have hopped up in bed right then and told him how crazy he was.

"I wonder how strong you really are. You're just like me: Ryder Pride. Neither of us can admit weakness or defeat. So how can I take you from this place when that might break you? You're tough, kid, but maybe not that tough." My dad sighed and put his head in his hands. "Then again, you might be.

"I wish I knew the right thing to do." Once more he gave a weary exhale. "I love you, Lex. No matter what, I will always love you." With a final, haggard sigh, my father stood up and made his way out of the room.

As soon as he was gone, I released a breath and my astral self disappeared from the bed. Closing my eyes, I began to remove my ceremonial clothes. Thinking through this all very careful-ly, I changed into my pajamas.

Sometimes the best medicine for a big prob-lem is to just meditate and let it go. So that's what I did. Opening the casements, I sat by the window and breathed the comforting scent of ivy as I cleared my mind. If I could do nothing about a situation, there was no point in worrying about it. I had to believe that, or I would lose my mind.

Of all the things I wanted to do the following morning, seeing my dad downstairs wasn't one of them. It was the weekend, meaning that he had time to spend with his family. Mostly he worked out on Sunday, but he'd been watching me like a hawk yesterday as I'd gotten ready for my date.

Today was our traditional family day. After last night, I was not looking forward to this. After all the things he said, how could I be at all comfortable with him today?

I got lucky. My dad seemed just as uncomfortable with me. Following my routine, I'd gotten up, taken a shower, and went to the piano for my two-hour practice. While I was doing that, his own Ryder Pride seemed to kick in and he came to talk to me.

I tried not to flinch as Dad sat down on the bench beside me while I played. It took all of the skill I'd acquired not to mess up the piece I was working on. I wasn't an Alyssa Rice, but I had enough discipline to win a recital or two. Which, at this point, seemed all my dad could think about as he reached out a hand and took hold of my right wrist. I stopped instantly.

"Why did you want to learn to play, Lex? The truth?" His voice was quiet, as it had been last night. It was so weird seeing my dad like this. I guess now he considered me grown up enough to show me he was more than just my protector. It made me smile.

"The truth?" I asked slyly, making my dad raise an eyebrow. "Ryder Pride."

That made him look at me in confusion, but it put a smile on his face as well.

"When we first moved in, I was intimidated

by it, in a way. I don't do too well with being intimidated, so I decided that I had to learn to play it."

As I spoke, my dad studied me in a careful, almost suspicious manner. "Alyssa Rice was a musical prodigy." He said it to gauge my reaction.

I didn't even flinch. "I know. And if you remember, I asked Mom about me playing before I ever learned about Alyssa Rice."

"Are you saying she had no effect on your reason for continuing to play?" My dad knew how to hit a point.

"Dad, I'm not playing because Alyssa can't play anymore. I play because I am just like you. Ryder Pride. Once I start something, I stick with it. Alyssa or no Alyssa, I'm still playing."

"Is she the reason you do anything? At all?"

That one made me stop and think. I mean, obviously Alyssa affected what I did. I was more cautious with my magick and I paid closer attention to what Morgan said. My approach to spirits was much less cavalier, seeing as how her past wasn't exactly what a helpful nine-year-old could hope for. In all, the only way she affected my decisions was in an area of my life my dad couldn't know about.

I took a deep breath before looking my dad in the eye. "Dad, Alyssa will always affect my life. But I'm strong enough to decide *how* she affects it. I don't live my life for her. Alyssa's moved on. So have I. If other people don't understand that, that's their problem."

A small smile appeared on my dad's face. Standing up, he grabbed both sides of my face and kissed my forehead. I laughed as he let go. One of his hands lingered on my face and he smiled at me for a minute more.

"I love you, Lexi Girl."

"I love you too, Dad."

He kissed my forehead one last time before he left the room. With a relieved sigh, I turned back to the piano and continued my practice in a much better mood.

As soon as I was able, I headed for Morgan's. I had to tell her what happened on my date. Even more than the gushy, girly stuff. She had to know about the instinctive magick. Could it have been caused by my upcoming Ascension?

My instincts? Something was going on. This year, it was going to get big. I could feel it.

When I got to Morgan's however, I had two very big surprises waiting for me. Faylin and Fiona. They were standing in the driveway, apparently waiting for me, since Morgan hadn't even left the house.

Riding up, I noticed that the gargoyles didn't feel the negativity at all emanating from the twins. An indication of where their loyalties lay. When it came to the twins, they'd never be kept out. Sarah was leaning against her sister's car, her arms crossed as she glared at the house. Anne was sitting on the hood one moment before pacing around the next. Instead of furious, she looked worried.

You know your daughters are here, right? I sent the message to Morgan and listened for the reply.

They are waiting on you. I thought it best not to disturb them while they are so agitated. Despite her words, Morgan seemed a little amused at my predicament.

Ugh. I want to talk to you. Not them.

So come talk to me and then deal with them. You are more than capable of slipping past them undetected.

I smiled at that one and sighed. Blending in with my surroundings was much harder to do in the daylight, but I managed. Perhaps the scary part was that I managed so well. My Ascension date was getting closer and closer, it felt like.

After hopping the fence, instead of attempting to open the gate undetected, I strolled to the front door. They might have seen the door open, but since they couldn't see me, neither came to investigate. As soon as the door was closed, I dropped the invisibility.

"How long have they been out there?"

"Which time? They waited a couple of hours for you yesterday, until they deigned to disturb me in the garden. I told them that you were probably spending time with your family and that you did not spend every second with me, contrary to popular belief."

I smiled at that one. It was so true. And I couldn't blame her. Why should she help out the twins if they were just there to badger me? So now it was up to me to deal with them, after I debriefed her.

"Why are they here, Alexandria?"

"That's why I'm here," I sighed as I sat down.

Quickly, I explained everything that had happened and what I thought could have caused it.

Morgan had other ideas.

"How clear has your mind been as of late, Lex?"

Right then, my eyes narrowed in suspicion. She only ever called me 'Lex' when it was something a little bit more personal. So, a clear mind had little to do with my magick malfunction. The one personal thing in my life that had changed was Matt. It didn't take a genius to see what she was implying.

"Not that clear," I admitted. "Matt has made it a little harder to focus lately."

Morgan smiled. "Remember what I said about living in both worlds?"

"Yes."

"This is why I said it. My daughters–*all* of my daughters–had the same problem when they found themselves becoming fond of someone. They focused less on their magick but everything seemed to happen naturally. Instinctively. It was the breakups that caused their magick to go haywire. I guess that means being in love–even crazy in love–is good for magick."

"And for you? Were you crazy in love and instinctive in magick?"

There was an unidentifiable glint in Morgan's eyes as she answered, "Yes."

A silence fell then, as there was nothing left to say. Then the pacing outside grew closer and closer to the door. Anne had sensed me and I smiled at Morgan.

"What do you think? Should I let them suffer a little longer?" I asked with a grin.

"Depends on how long you want them lingering outside. For me, though I love my daughters, they are not the most hospitable of creatures. I would prefer their hostility to leave my garden as soon as possible."

At the mention of the garden, I shot to my feet. "I'll be back. Then we'll heal the plants again."

Morgan smiled as I reached the door. With a last roll of my eyes, I went back outside to face Anne and her sister.

"Anne. Fay." If Sarah was going to be hostile with me, I would show her no mercy.

"Our kids saw you!" Faylin snarled at me. I was taken aback at the ferocity in her tone and my eyes shot to Anne.

"Nathan wasn't there."

"Mark and Tyler were both there with dates. It was Tyler who..."

"Threw the drink at me."

"I'm sorry," Anne said quietly.

Faylin stood on her sister's left, shaking her head at me. "I tried to warn you, but you wouldn't listen. You chose this for yourself."

"Just like you chose it, Sarah? People who tell their kids that are the reason we grew up miserable," Anne growled at her sister, fire flashing in her eyes.

"We didn't choose to be the witch's daughters, either. There's a difference."

"Yeah," I snapped, "I have the backbone to deal with it. I don't care what those idiot kids say or do. They're ignorant." My gaze bored into Anne's as I added, "Ignorance can be remedied with the right teachings."

"Certainly sounds like you care," Faylin remarked.

I could feel my temperature running high. My skin was burning as my blood began to boil. She did not know who she was dealing with.

"It doesn't matter to me what they do because I can take care of myself. But I wouldn't wish this on someone else."

"Then *stop this!*" Faylin pleaded.

"I can't," I snapped back, furious that this was still something they were pushing.

"If you would only try–"

"Then what? I'm not as pathetic as you. Magick chose me, and I will not turn away from it."

"Pathetic? You think it is pathetic to be able to step away from an addiction? Try it, Alex, and see how it comes to define you."

I had just opened my mouth to deliver a retort when Anne stepped between us and snapped, "Enough!"

"Get her out of here, Anne. I won't do anything to her around Morgan, but if she keeps testing me..." It was an empty threat, but they didn't need to know that.

The look Anne gave me was nothing short of vicious. "And that's how it starts. The minute you do something to her, you won't be able to stop from doing something to someone else. Be careful with even your thoughts, Alex," she hissed. Turning back to her sister, she pushed her toward the car.

Whirling away, Faylin got into the vehicle. Anne turned back to me and took a deep breath to calm herself. I was beyond that, I was so angry. Just closing my eyes and taking a deep breath wasn't going to work this time.

"Alex, my son and my nephew saw you perform instinctive magick. Sarah's daughter was also there. The remarks and accusations against you... I can't stop Tyler from being mean to you. Sarah's daughter is going to be even more hostile with you than you are with Sarah. This is a warning, Alex. Stop. Now," Anne pleaded.

In my anger, I couldn't hear the words she spoke with any form of open-mindedness. "Anne, I don't need or want your warning. If you think I can be intimidated by one event of instinctive magick, you are out of your mind. Unlike your sister, I can and will keep from getting burned by my magick."

Anne sighed and turned away. Right before she got in the car however, she looked back over her shoulder at me. "Not all flames reside in magick, Alexandria. Make sure you don't get burned by the ones in this world as well."

Chapter Twelve

UTTERLY MUNDANE

I didn't stick around Morgan's long after that. It was impossible to do anything other than make matters worse. So, right after the twins were gone, I took my bike and headed for the end of Old Grove Road.

The weather was cooler for July. It showed signs of raining later and a wind was swaying the trees. No one would be at the lake. At least, no one should be. I wanted time to calm down. Time to be with the ghosts of my past. Those, at least, I could deal with. I could pity them. Feel sorry for them. That would make me much less sorry for myself. As pathetic as that was–using them for that–it was the only thing I could take comfort in right now.

When I got to the lake, it was empty. I ditched

my bike without bothering to protect it. My mind needed protection so much more than my bike at that point.

With a rush I couldn't explain, my feet were well on their way into entering the water. The air around me seemed to thrum with the magick. I was drowning in it. Losing myself to the sensations and vibrations. I couldn't breathe. My vision was spinning. Something was happening.

I spun in place and my vision turned into the bright white of a sunny day. I saw myself with Matt, standing on the beach as we prepared to go swimming. We were holding hands.

Another spin. Matt and I were walking down a street, eating ice cream.

Another spin. I was playing my piano and watched Matt walk up from the gate. He stopped to watch me through the window. I smiled and played for him.

Another spin and I was starting to hear Victoria's Lullaby playing in my ears. The water sloshed around my legs and I could feel the silt between my toes. The visions continued to hit me and my breath came in gasps.

Finally, I stopped and opened my eyes, seeing

clearly for the first time.

We stood on the shore holding hands. Kids came up behind us and started calling names, demanding I do something to them. Curse them. They taunted me until Matt got in a fight with them.

Walking down the street, someone bumped into me on purpose. No instinctive magick that time. Matt got into another fight on my behalf.

Even coming to my house. I began to play Victoria's Lullaby and was lost in a vision that ruined my time with him.

For every vision I had of me happy, I also saw myself hurt and upset. Because of my magick.

I fell into the water, soaking my clothes as I cried. Taking a fist, I smashed it into the liquid, destroying my reflection over and over again before it had time to materialize. I didn't cry. I didn't have hysterics. But right then, I was losing my mind.

And I understood what Anne meant.

If I let magick into every part of my life—even the parts it had no business being in—then I could only expect to be affected in every area of my life by it. Magick was my cause and people's reactions my effect. I could not have one without the other. By keeping my magick to myself, I'd avoided just those kinds of disturbances. After the other night...

Understood. Some parts of my life would have to remain mundane.

The images started to shift and change, flowing through the water as my reflection tried to form. No fighting. Just stares. Mean comments. And one look from me shutting everyone up. No magick. Just people. Just normal. Just me and Matt.

No. Really. When the water settled enough that I could see everything as it was, Matt's reflection was right beside mine. He looked so concerned that it just made the situation worse. I didn't want him to see me like this.

"Alex? Are you okay?" Matt asked in a worried, quiet voice.

To make matters worse, he waded into the water where I'd fallen and grabbed my arms, soaking his own jeans and sneakers. I couldn't answer. My embarrassment, anger, and anguish were making it almost impossible to breathe, much less speak. To get it over with, I allowed

Matt to lead me out of the water and up onto the shore. I didn't get much further from the water's edge before collapsing onto a fallen log. Matt sat beside me and wrapped his arm around my shoulders. I couldn't help it as I leaned into his shoulder and cried.

"Alex," Matt crooned as he stroked my hair and made shushing noises.

At last, the tears started to ebb. I was getting to the sniffling phase and tried to wipe my eyes before Matt could get another good look at my face. Already my eyes felt swollen and I could only guess how red they were. That was too many blows for one day. To have Matt witness my breakdown was just one more solid landing to the gut.

"Are you okay? What happened?"

I shook my head. "Nothing. I'm fine. Really." I was much better at telling half-truths than outright lies.

"No, you're not. What happened, Alex? Please tell me?"

I sighed. He was going to find out eventually.

"You saw it. The other night. What I did." Matt nodded in answer. "Well, you're not the only one. The chances of this making me even more of public enemy number one just skyrocketed. Which also puts you in the crosshairs. I can't stand the thought of something happening to you just because I can do things that aren't considered normal. Because I am not average, I am to be punished for it. And you as well, if you still want to be seen with me."

The look of outrage that clouded his features was instantaneous.

"If?" he demanded. "You honestly think I'm like those other jerks? That I'd just dump you and walk away because you're *different*? After what happened in that movie theater, you still think I'm capable of walking away like nothing happened?"

Fresh tears were brimming in my eyes, but for a different reason now.

"You really don't care?" I could only manage a whisper.

"No, Alex. Why would I? Why *should* I?"

I had to look away. Wipe my eyes. Smile. "I don't know."

We sat in silence for a moment. Long enough to hear thunder begin a steady roll in the clouds above our heads, causing us both to look up and see the faint flashes of lightning higher up in the atmosphere. After a minute, as the first drops began drifting down from the sky, I finally met Matt's eyes.

They were so dark and deep, it felt like I was looking into a pit. Only, instead of vipers at the bottom, I was seeing a flame. It burned with curiosity and emotion. With the potential to burn me alive, I could tell this flame was only meant to bring me out of my cold, empty world. Give me some life.

"Did you really think me capable of abandoning you like that?" The words seemed simple enough; a straight-forward question. But not at all what he was asking.

"No. I knew you wouldn't. Not once would you back down because of me. Which made me feel that much worse. You can't fight the world because I'm a witch, Matt. It doesn't work that way."

A sly, crooked smile inched onto his face as he disregarded my admission. "Who said anything about fighting?"

Right then, I knew that he knew that I knew

something. Instead of answering, I gave him a withering look that he broke into a grin over. We both knew that he would have gotten in a fight over me. An act of stupidity that I was unable to condone.

"C'mon. We should get you home," Matt said as the rain began to come down harder and faster. I gave it another fifteen minutes before it became a downpour.

"We better hurry. I know a shortcut from here."

Together, the two of us stood up and stepped over the log as we went to retrieve our bikes. In an unspoken agreement, we grabbed the bikes and walked them onto the trail that led all the way through the woods and came out right by my house. It was the same trail that led to Morgan's, if I was to go straight through the woods. But from the lake, there was a distinct angle that left us only a mile to travel rather than the three that would have us traveling around the normal way.

Our walk began in silence. Each of us listened to the steady patter of raindrops hitting verdant green leaves before making their way down to us. With every single step, it sounded and felt like the rain was increasing. Then, in that sudden way every good storm promises, it started to pour. Even the trees couldn't protect us.

Running alongside bikes wasn't the most co-ordinated thing in the world. Running alongside bikes alongside another person was even more complicated. Somehow we managed. All the way, we laughed like crazy as the rain pelted us.

Who would ever have thought being so mundane could be so much fun?

Matt and I made it to my house in record timing. We were still laughing when we rolled the bikes across the road and leaned them against the front gate. Before I had a chance to unlatch it, Matt picked me up from behind and spun in tight circles until we were back in the middle of the road. I flung my head back and laughed at the sky, watching as the storm churned above the treetops.

When he set me back down, we stumbled back to the gate. For one long moment, we leaned against the wood and stared at each other. The question sat between us, though neither of us was going to say it aloud. Whether he stayed or went, it was up to him. At the same time, whether I wanted him to stay or go was up to me. Then his expression changed and I had my answer.

Smiling slightly, Matt opened the gate for me so I could take my bike through, but I knew he wasn't planning on staying. After parking my bike on the path, I turned back around to face him. That's when he did it.

The rain beat a pounding rhythm into our faces. That didn't matter. Water cooled our hot skin. We didn't notice. Being soaked to our bones didn't even faze us.

All that mattered was his lips on mine. My first kiss. In that moment when I turned around, Matt had stepped close to me without a hint of hesitation. I was impressed by his confidence for a moment before he put his hand on the side of my neck and leaned in. I'd closed my eyes the minute I felt his soft lips on mine. It felt right.

When Matt's hand slipped from my throat and he stepped back, I took in a deep breath through my nose and let it out as I opened my eyes. The smile on my face could not get any wider. Nothing could be more perfect than that.

Matt was smiling triumphantly as he stood in the gateway. He had one hand on the post and the other on the open gate. After a second, he drew the gate closer to him, reinforcing the impression that he had to go. Something I wasn't too happy about.

"I'll see you later," Matt said in a low voice.

I nodded. "See you."

I was just turning away when I heard him call my name. When I turned back the gate cut us off but Matt was leaning on it and I stepped closer. He motioned me even closer. When I was almost leaning against the gate myself, he leaned forward and stole another kiss. Before I could respond, Matt stepped away and winked at me before getting on his bike and taking off.

Chapter Thirteen

LOVELY MAGICK

I was so happy, I almost left my bike. After a minute, I had to turn around and run it to the shed. Once it was put up, I stepped back out into the pouring rain. Instead of running through the rain like I'd intended, I soon found myself spinning in it. Round and round, getting hit repeatedly by cold drops, I danced my way straight to the kitchen door.

Once inside, I had to stop and drip onto the clean floor for a little bit. I'd clean it up later. Right now, my head was spinning too much and I barely restrained myself from doing a happy dance right there. After a minute of leaning against the door, I shoved off of it and went in search of my mother. I knew she would love to hear about this!

"Mom?" I called, expecting her to come out of her office. Instead, I heard her voice in the parlor and rushed right to her without bothering to wonder who she was talking to.

"Hey Lex. I–" She didn't get further than that. I didn't allow it.

"Matt kissed me!" I squealed. My mother's jaw dropped and I didn't bother to stop the words falling from my lips as I described what had happened at the gate. I ignored that she wasn't as excited, though she couldn't dispel of a telling smile, as much as she was trying to get me to stop talking.

"Alexandria!" she finally exhaled in amused exasperation. I stopped on a dime, feeling confused. Then she moved slightly to the side so I could see a bunch of people in the other room. Each one wore a slight, amused smile. "We have guests."

My eyes grew wide and I clapped my hands over my mouth. "I'm sorry! I didn't realize. I'll let you get back... It was nice to see you all," I stammered in embarrassment as an unfamiliar blush lit up my face. Turning on my heel, I rushed up the stairs and went straight to my room. I collapsed, laughing, onto my bed.

It was one of those times that I seriously hated not having any friends. I wanted to tell someone. Anyone! My mom was busy. Morgan had just seen me. There was no one else.

Heck. The only other person to talk to me without fear rolling off of them was Nathan. I wasn't going to talk about Matt with him. Talking to him about my boyfriend would be too weird.

Once I thought the word, I felt like something wiped my brain clear. It wasn't something I had ever thought of. I was too weird to have friends. Obviously, I was too weird for a boyfriend, too. But Matt was my boyfriend. I could not believe it. There was finally someone who was able to look at all of the weird, creepy, unusual, and magickal things about me and still wanted me.

Sometime toward the end of my reverie, I became aware of the shivering. At first, I had assumed that it was from excitement. After a few minutes, I remembered the downpour that had soaked me clear through to my skin. So, I got up and headed for a hot shower. When I was done, I gathered together my bedding and threw the comforters in the washing machine. From my closet I retrieved the other set of bedding and made my bed-with only a little magickal influence.

It was maybe an hour later that my mom found me in the kitchen, mopping up my watery trail with a grin on my face. She stood in the doorway for about five minutes with a wide smile before coming and interrupting me by grabbing my face and kissing me on the forehead.

"Mom," I pretended to grumble.

"I am the envy of mothers everywhere. Which of them has a daughter who cleans up after herself without being told to?"

"None. Because I'm just that special," I responded grandly.

"You will find no disagreement in this house," she laughed with me as she moved to sit on one of the stools by the island. I finished mopping up before turning back to her.

"Was it that bad after my … announcement?" I asked while fighting a grin. I failed.

"Not at all. Well, let's put it this way, you wouldn't have wanted to be in the room. You'd probably have third degree burns from all of the blushing."

I was blushing now just hearing about it.

"Yup. Just like that," my mom commented, grinning as she pointed out my red face.

I ducked my head but grinned in response. Thank Goddess for Ryder Pride! If I'd been like other girls, I'd probably be throwing an embarrassed tantrum. Instead, I let my mother have her fun. How often did she get to pick on me for something like this?

"So, now that we're alone, do I get the full disclosure?" she asked, folding her hands over her crossed knees and staring at me speculatively.

I needed no further invitation. Sitting on the stool beside my mom, I gushed everything to her. Even the fact that I had been a crying mess when Matt found me-a fact I swore her to secrecy over so that my dad wouldn't find out. And she felt all the right emotions and said all the right things as I spilled all of the safe details.

For the next few hours, my mom and I talked like we used to. I know it made her feel good, me confiding in her like this. It felt good to me, too. I guess what really made me love it was the fact that I now had something I could talk to her about. Before, magick ruled my world. Now, things were gaining a bit of a balance. At last.

The next day, it was still pouring. However, that didn't stop me from going to Morgan's. Matt had called and said that his mom was making him stay at home, so I took that opportunity to fill her in. Of course, it was in astral form, so I didn't physically leave the house. While I sat and played the piano, another me was spilling everything to Morgan-magickal and otherwise.

The day following, Matt called to ask me out on another date. It took just as much coercion to get my dad to agree the second time as it had the first time. He was okay with his daughter having one date. It was something entirely out of his realm of understanding for his thirteen-year-old daughter to have a boyfriend. After all, this wasn't supposed to happen for another two years. But it was happening now and the same rules applied: I was going with or without his permission.

The date was set and I spent a glorious day just bouncing around in excitement. Granted, at thirteen, there's not a lot of date ideas. But the carnival was in the next town over and I had a pretty good idea what he had in store for me.

I was right. Matt and I were driven there by my mom-his mom had heard about me and was too leery about the date, but his dad had given him the go-ahead to date me because 'it's all a load of bull' and 'what town gets its kicks by spreading rumors about a kid?' Despite the reservations our parents had, the two of us had a great time at the carnival. We kissed again on the Ferris wheel, ensuring it was a night to remember.

In the weeks following, all of my nights started to do that. Run in this awesome, endless stream of good occurrences. My days with him at the lake. My afternoons with him in town. And the date nights he always seemed to have planned every week. So much of my time was spent with Matt, even I couldn't believe it.

Toward the end of July, I had a piano recital. I was more than excited when he came with my parents-who ended up loving him. Or, at least my mom ended up loving him. My dad, on the other hand, wasn't so much of a fan. Since Matt had yet to even hold my hand in his presence, however, he got a tentative stamp of approval.

It wasn't until August second that it really started to become clear to me what I was feeling for Matt.

We were walking through the woods, having chosen not to take our bikes down to the lake. Our fingers were linked together and we took turns leading each other along the path. I knew it better, but Matt was at home in the woods. A fact that I appreciated.

Suddenly, I felt a slight tugging as Matt tripped on a tree root. He didn't realize I saw him catch himself, before he allowed himself to fall, pulling me to the ground with him.

Shoving his shoulder, I exclaimed, "You did that on purpose!"

"I tripped!"

I rolled my eyes at him to let him know I wasn't buying it, but I stayed where I was. We laid side by side and stared up into the canopy of trees. Everything was vibrant green and flowing in a soft breeze. Together, we watched in silence as birds flew across the sky and squirrels jumped between the trees. Everything was magical in its own right.

That was the first time I felt it. The stirring to show Matt something magickal. Something he had never seen before. More than an instinctive shield, I wanted to show him how special I was. To prove that I wasn't a freak. To prove that I was worth dating. I was worth the problems that our relationship had caused him-he never told me about them, but I wasn't an idiot.

In order to do all that, though, it'd have to be something convincing. Special. But what? What could I do to convince him that I was just a girl with extraordinary gifts?

"Matt?" I murmured, turning my head to face him.

He smiled as he turned toward me. "Lex?" he mimicked, causing me to smile too.

"Can I show you something?"

I guess my tone alerted him to something because he leaned up on his elbows and looked down at me. His expression was questioning, but there was a gleam in his eye that was not only curious, but excited. I took that as consent.

Turning my head back to look at the sky, I motioned him to lie back down. Matt did as I asked and I bit my lip over my excited grin.

"Just keep looking up," I whispered. Already I was grounding and centering, my mind taking on the blankness that allowed my magick to flow into whatever I wished. Of course, my plan had a serious potential of backlash-he could freak out-but I was going off past experience and figured he would realize that it was just me.

Glamours were simple to make. They were just a lie for the eyes. And all I was doing was taking a previously studied scene and changing it. For now.

A few feet above our heads and all around us, the sky darkened into the dim of twilight. Stars appeared in our view and the woods seemed to grow darker. The moon shone down on us, lightening the world around us and I saw Matt's eyes grow wide as he turned to look at me. Without acknowledging him, I allowed sunrise to kiss the sky and his head whipped back and forth as the dimness disappeared to reveal a world full of color.

It was autumn in my world. Scarlet and gold leaves lay around us and the sky was lit up with the colors of fire. Orange and yellow flared up around the bright red. A few leaves dislodged themselves from the trees and drifted down toward us. Before they reached us, however, they turned to snow and the trees became barren, covered in the weighty, frozen water.

Matt's mouth was ajar as a full moon rose over our winter surroundings, leaving everything in a stark contrast of dark woods and white snow. New constellations were in the sky, but were hardly visible due to that moon.

A spring morning dawned and fresh, green shoots popped out of the ground while the trees were revealing their own sparkling new coats. Then there were the wildflowers that sprang up in the woods as we inched back to our summer afternoon. In a way, it was the perfect year.

As time caught up with us, I let the glamour fall away and turned to see Matt watching me. A small smile fixed itself on my face as I waited for his reaction. Instead of saying anything, Matt leaned forward and kissed me on the lips. When he pulled back, he smiled at me but his eyes were filled to brimming with curiosity.

"Thank you. For showing me that. It was amazing."

I let out a relieved breath and smiled widely.

"You're welcome."

"How many people know you can do that?

I bit my lip. "Just me and Morgan. And now you."

"Your parents don't know?"

Shaking my head, I answered, "No. They wouldn't know how to handle that. My dad is too logical. Jarhead to the end. And my mom... She's a little more on the creative side, but she's a little naïve. I couldn't throw something like this on her. Especially after the Alyssa Rice thing."

"I was wondering ... can I ask you about that?" His voice was tentative.

"No." My answer was flat and immediate. Then I took a breath and explained. "Alyssa's story is over now. She's finally at rest. I'm not going to bring it all up again, in a sense. It's not my place to tell what happened to her. Do you get it?"

Matt nodded before looking at me with a sly grin. "But you know, don't you? The full story. The things no one even suspected. You know what really happened."

I nodded, daring not to put the answer into words.

"I think that might be what I like most about you. That you know things but you don't throw it in people's faces."

A faint heat crept into my cheeks and I imagined my features had taken on a pink tinge. "I like that you're so accepting. You don't freak out over what I can do. And that makes me feel so relieved." The words came out in little more than a whisper and I kept my eyes trained on the skyline.

Matt reached over and pushed a strand of hair off my face, forcing my eyes to meet his. Once more, he leaned over and kissed me. This time he didn't pull away until two minutes later.

That was when it hit me. I was in puppy love.

Chapter Fourteen

AWKWARD MOMENTS

"Dad, can I talk to you?" I still wasn't sure about this, but at this point I had already committed myself to this course of action.

"Of course, Lexi Girl. What's on your mind?" he asked as he turned away from the mirror. He'd just gotten home from work and was busy changing into civilian clothes.

Taking a deep breath, I spouted the words with my next exhale. "I think I'm in puppy love."

There wasn't a lot that could catch my dad off guard, but this was one of the few things that could do it. Without even looking at me, he stepped back and sunk onto the bed before dropping his head into his hands. I took that opportunity to ease into the room and close the door behind me.

With his head still in his hands, my dad grumbled, "Aw, Lex. You're growing up way too fast for me. Don't you want to talk to your mom about this?" He raised his head to give me a pleading look, begging me not to force him into seeing me as a teenager instead of his Lexi Girl. It made me smile a little.

"No way. You know mom. Total hopeless romantic," I said as I went to sit on the bed beside him. It was easier for me, too, if I wasn't having a total eye-contact conversation. I may have looked like my mother, but I was *his* daughter through and through.

"Mom would blow this way out of proportion. She'd be trying to stir up some fairy tale romance in my head with all that happily-ever-after stuff. I'm not naïve, Dad. I know this isn't the stuff relationships are built upon. What I am feeling is really just ... puppy love."

My dad sighed beside me, as though preparing himself to actually have this conversation with his daughter. I couldn't even imagine what I was putting him through.

"Why are you so sure of that, Lex?" He made a pretty convincing effort at sounding supportive.

"I want to hang out with him all the time. Like, *all* the time. I feel like I can tell him things. I can be myself around him. But I'm always afraid that someone can change his mind about me. That someone can convince him that I'm not the person he's been seeing. And I hate that feeling. If I loved him like how you and mom love each other, then I would be able to trust that that would never happen. I would be able to trust him not to turn his back on me." At this point, what I needed more than anything was to say it aloud.

If I had tried to tell this to my mom, she would have tried to allay my fears. She'd have been convinced that I was blowing this way out of proportion and that I should just enjoy my time with him. Something I was incapable of doing.

My father and I sat in silence for several long minutes as I mulled things over. Then he sighed once more. "What do you want me to say, Lex?"

"I want you to tell me that this is normal! To tell me that this kind of thing happens to everyone," I found myself pleading as tears sprang into my eyes. "I don't know, Dad. That's why I came to you."

My dad wrapped his arms around me, enfolding me in a secure, steady embrace. I closed my eyes as I let him hold me, breathing in the scent of his body wash. More than anything, I needed that hug.

"Oh, Lexi Girl. Well, to be honest, old-fashioned puppy love isn't that normal anymore. I'm sure you know that more than anyone. All you kids these days are too eager to try adult things and–"

"Dad. Please stay on topic here. I really don't want to have that particular talk ever again," I grumbled. I felt him take another deep breath, his chest expanding and relaxing with the exhale.

"Alright. My point, Lex, is that ... well, baby girl you are *not* normal. Everything you've experienced, even up to this point, is not something everyone goes through. But that's all made you tough as nails, with an annoying belief that you can handle everything yourself. Lex, you're one of the most perceptive people I know, and you know how to look at things without any form of covering over those pretty blue eyes." He tilted my chin up so he could see into those eyes.

"So, you're saying that what I'm feeling isn't average," I sighed, looking away.

"Now I didn't say that. I just said that you are not average. What you're feeling, though, sounds like good, clean puppy love to me. The kind every thirteen-year-old girl dreams about, I imagine. Of course, I suppose most of them would take your mother's view on things." Dad grinned at me and squeezed my sides a little.

After a minute, I stood up and threw my arms around his neck. "Thank you, Dad. That was exactly what I needed to hear."

"You're welcome, Lexi Girl," he replied as I stepped away from him.

"I'll see you at dinner," I said as I headed for the door.

"Going to compare notes with your mother now?" I turned my head at his voice, seeing a knowing grin on his face.

I raised an eyebrow. "And let Mom know I talked to you about this before her? No thanks, I like my head where it is."

We shared a laugh as I made good my escape.

Some things never change. Including the relationship I had with my dad.

Or so I thought.

Chapter Fifteen

PREPARING

A week later, the moment I had been waiting all summer for had arrived. I awoke with my blood staining the inside of my thighs and a weight settled around my shoulders. With my first period, I would gain the full extent of my power.

I pondered on that throughout my shower, amazed by how bodily fluids could focus magick to an almost immeasurable degree. Blood being the most powerful, of course. Being that it was period blood I was spilling, it was also a bit of a fertility pledge as well. It would draw the power right to me.

As I was getting dressed, I could feel the enormity of the situation pressing in on me. The amount of preparation I had to accomplish would be time consuming. What I needed to get done before that, however, would set me on edge. I didn't know if I could play it cool in front of my parents long enough to get the permission I sought.

After spending a flurried amount of time on the piano, I couldn't even force myself to make it through my two-hour practice session. I was in such a frenzied mood that I couldn't make myself sit there for another minute trying to read the music and stick to the piece I was to perform for my next recital. After one terrible hour of practice, I got to my feet and sought out my mother.

"Hey, Lex. Done so soon?" she asked as she prepared snacks for her book club. (I still got red-faced whenever I thought about them.)

"Yeah. It's a new piece and I can't seem to focus. I think a breather is in order."

"I agree. That thing hasn't gotten a day of rest for the past three years," she replied with a smile. Her blue eyes lit up like glowing sapphires and her amusement was contagious, causing me to grin in response.

"Well, it's gonna get it. Do you mind if I

spend the night at Morgan's?"

"Really? You haven't stayed over there since the summer started. Is it alright with her?"

"I'm sure it is. I'll call over there and ask as soon as you give me an answer." I grinned because we both already knew what she would say.

My mom rolled her eyes and spent a few minutes pretending to think about it. "Fine."

"Thanks, Mom," I said and kissed her on the cheek. Then I grabbed the cordless phone and carried it into the other room in order to pretend to call her.

As soon as I was out of sight of my mom–and out of hearing range–I cast out an astral projection into Morgan's house. I found Morgan sitting in her chair, sipping at more tea. She looked up upon feeling me there and raised a single eyebrow.

"It's tonight," I stated. I waited until I saw understanding flash in her eyes before I called back my other self. I still had a lot left to do before I could be close to ready for tonight.

First things first: see Matt.

He was already at the lake by the time I got there. I'd left my bike at home, seeing as I planned on going straight to Morgan's. Everything I needed was in my backpack. After spotting his bike off to the side where I normally parked mine, I couldn't help but wonder how long he had been there.

"No bike today?" he asked as soon as he noticed me on the trail. His eyebrows rose when he saw the backpack. "And I'm guessing that's not filled with just a towel."

I smiled. Chalk one up to the other number of things I liked about Matt: he was observant. "I'm spending the night at Morgan's."

Matt nodded and an amused look came into his eyes. "Is that why you wanted to see me so early?"

"Sort-of. I figure I've got a few hours of free time. Beyond that, my time belongs to my mentor." Unconsciously, I looked out over the lake and saw Victoria's last walk one more time. Then Freyja's final journey filled my vision and I forced myself to look away.

Matt met my eyes with a serious gaze. Curiosity laced through his irises but it was obvious he was suppressing it. "You okay?"

Forcing a smile, I nodded. "Fine."

Raising another eyebrow, Matt obviously doubted my assertion. "What's going on, Lex? Is something going to happen tonight?"

I took a deep breath and let it out in a sigh before sitting down on the fallen log facing the lake. Matt sat beside me but his eyes never left my face. I had to think very carefully about what I was going to tell him.

"Yes. Something is going to happen tonight. Something magickal. It's going to be big. Matt, the last time something this big happened to me ... I changed. Aged. It's taken me four years to catch up to my own mentality and I'm still not even done doing that yet. After tonight... Matt, I might not be the same *person* tomorrow that I am today."

I looked away and closed my eyes after admitting that to him. In response, Matt moved closer to me and wrapped an arm around my shoulders. Smiling, I allowed my body to mold into his as I looked back up at him.

"You still gonna like me tomorrow?"

My smile widened and I pretended to think about it. "I'm not sure..."

Matt's other hand found its way to my side

and I jumped a little as he began to tickle me. Grinning, Matt asked in a slow, deliberate tone, "Are you still going to like me tomorrow?"

I squirmed as I laughed but he kept me where I was by the arm around my shoulders. My Ryder Pride urged me to deny it and free myself, proving to be the victor. But something that had come from my mother told me to let him have this moment. That proving to be the winner in every situation wasn't always worth it. Sometimes the reward was in just giving in to temptation.

"Yes! Yes!" I called out while laughing. "I will still like you tomorrow."

Matt stopped tickling me in an instant and I turned my head to look at him, pushing my brown hair back behind my ear. Smiling, he raised his left hand to brush his fingers along the right side of my face. "Good."

My own blue eyes sparked with Ryder Pride as I demanded, "Will *you* still like *me* tomorrow?"

Matt answered with a smile and a look in those warm brown eyes that said I should know better. His real answer followed when his lips met mine.

Matt and I were sitting there, making out

for five minutes before we heard someone clear their throat behind us. I gasped and my hand flew to cover my mouth as I turned toward the lake. My face turned scarlet in an instant as I stared out over the gray water. Now that I was paying attention, I didn't need to look to know who it was.

"Hey," Matt said in greeting. He sounded only a tiny bit uncomfortable, but I could tell how surprised he was when he ran a hand through his hair.

"Hey," Nathan replied, his voice a flat monotone.

Taking a deep breath, I prepared myself to face him. It shouldn't have been so hard. He was barely my friend. But he *was* my friend, and the one person who'd stuck by me for four years. This situation made me feel guilty about not telling him. I mean, he had known Matt and I were together. But I wasn't the one to tell him, and that made me feel like a coward.

"Hey. What're you doing here?" I asked in a voice that failed at sounding casual. "It's going to start raining in about an hour."

Nathan didn't even look away to check the

sky for my assessment. He didn't look anywhere but in my eyes. I couldn't meet his gaze and my eyes darted away.

"I was looking for you, actually."

There was a spike in his feeling of determination and it triggered enough alarm in me that my eyes shot to his, all of my embarrassment melted away in an instant. Without realizing, I was on my feet, my eyes boring into his as I walked right up to him.

"Why? What happened?" I demanded.

Nathan took a deep breath; his gaze moved away from my eyes for a minute and I noticed that he was doing his best to ignore Matt. What *that* was about, I had no idea. Right now, it didn't matter.

Meeting my eyes, Nathan said the words in his next exhale. "I think I was just fired." For the first time, I could hear the confusion in his voice.

My head jerked back in surprise and an incredulous look found its way upon my face. "What?"

Nathan exhaled again and it was like we were alone. "I don't know what happened. I stopped by the house and she was waiting for me at the gate. I handed her the mail and she gave me an envelope. Alex, it's three times as much as she normally pays me." The fact that Nathan was worried about this had me in a panic.

"What did she say, Nathan? Her words exactly?"

"Nothing! She just said that she *enjoyed* my 'visits' and that I didn't have to come back if I didn't want to. Alex, what's going on?"

My panic faded to be replaced by a slight worry. I couldn't help the glance back at Matt and his confusion seemed to ease a little bit. When I looked back at Nathan, however, his face was a thunderhead.

"You know what's going on, Lex? Tell me," Nathan demanded.

I was so used to my parents and Matt calling me 'Lex' that, at first, it didn't even register when Nathan did it. When I did notice, my mouth dropped. But Nathan was still giving me that angry, demanding look that made me shake my head and got me back on topic. Once more, I glanced back at Matt.

"Nathan, I wouldn't worry too much about

it. Morgan and I have something planned for tonight. I'm not sure what all is going to happen, but..."

"But it's something big enough that she's telling me that I don't have to come back? I'm not buying, Alex. She looked me in the eye and talked like she was going to die." His words came out rougher with emotion, which surprised me.

"I'll talk to her. I promise," I said in a soothing voice, reaching out a hand and touching his shoulder. Nathan sighed and nodded his head, refusing to meet my eyes. Smiling a little, I tried to get him to look at me as I said, "And if she tries any of that goodbye crap with me, I'll kick her witchy butt all the way to this lake."

It worked; a crooked, reluctant smile appeared on Nathan's face and he nodded. Another exhale brought more words. "Thanks. I just ... can't imagine Cedar Creek without her."

I raised an eyebrow. "How do you think I'll feel? I actually know *and* like her."

Nathan nodded and once more avoided my gaze. "Yeah." That was all he said.

Perhaps the reason this conversation was so weird was because Nathan always needed a large amount of determination to go near the house. Especially when he learned that Morgan was a real witch. It was hard for him to be near her. Though now, I understood something I'd been missing.

Nathan cared about Morgan.

I guess that might have been why I almost gave all three of us a heart attack when I wrapped my arms around Nathan in a hug. "It'll be okay, Nathan. Morgan's fine," I murmured. After a minute, Nathan patted my back and I could feel the awkwardness in his emotions spike. Since it was awkward for me too, I let go.

"Well, I'll see you later. Just promise me you'll let me know what's going on? And if I still have a job?"

I gave him a reassuring smile and nodded. "I'll let you know tomorrow. Come by the usual time?"

Nathan forced a crooked smile and nodded before walking away with his hands in his pockets. Honestly, I felt good about the encounter, though I was still surprised. At least I wasn't the only one who cared what happened to her. Which was more than I ever hoped for. Especially since

Nathan was her grandson. That was icing on the cake.

When Nathan got on his bike and headed back down the road, Matt came to stand beside me and I turned to see a questioning look on his face. My eyebrows pinched together and my head tilted to the side in an even more confused expression.

"Didn't know you guys were that close of friends," he commented.

"We're not," I answered.

"Really?" I nodded and Matt pressed his lips together a little bit. "Then what was *this* about?" Matt asked as he picked me up in a tight embrace. I laughed as he spun me around before setting me back on my feet.

"I don't know. He just looked like he could use it. To be honest, that is the longest conversation I've had with Nathan *ever*."

"Sounded like the strangest conversation you guys have ever had, too."

"Close enough. Definitely the most awkward."

"Agreed. Of course, since I wasn't really in the conversation..."

My eyes narrowed as I looked at Matt. There was a shadow in his eyes that he seemed to be trying to hide from me. But I was an empath, and that shadow in his eyes hid more than a shadow in his emotions. It made me smile.

"You know you don't have a reason to be jealous," I told him.

"I'm not jealous," he replied too quickly.

I could have pressed it, but that probably would have ticked him off. Instead I just said, "Good." Then I wrapped my arms around his neck and went back to kissing him.

Chapter Sixteen

ASCENSION

If I hadn't promised Nathan, I probably never would have broached the subject with Morgan. Just the fact that she could be saying goodbye... Though it seemed unlikely while talking to Nathan, doubts had wormed their way into my head and I didn't want to know anymore. But a promise is a promise.

"Nathan's worried about you," I stated in as casual a voice as I could manage.

"Is he now? Well that is unexpected," Morgan remarked while she turned the page in her Book of Shadows.

"That's what I thought. Apparently, the way you told him he didn't have to come back if he didn't want to made him think you were saying your last goodbye or something." I glanced askance at my teacher as I spoke. She didn't even blink an eye.

"Why should he have to come here if it makes him uncomfortable?"

"Why decide this now?" I countered. I didn't like the way she dodged the question.

Morgan smiled a little but still didn't look up at me. "You're here, my dear. I think it is time you began to decide what is needed and what is not. Perhaps you should start taking more responsibility for your home away from home." When she looked up at me, her lips were pulled into a smile but her eyes were blocking something. She even had her emotions hidden from me.

In fact, they had been blocked for some time. Only now was I focused enough to realize it. Being with Matt clouded my senses more than I had thought. No wonder he put me on edge when we first met. My instincts knew this would happen.

"Now I see why he's worried," I remarked. Nathan was right, something was seriously *off*.

"Neither of you should be worried." Too careful. The way she worded it, how it came out of her mouth, everything was too careful.

"Morgan, what's going to happen tonight?" I demanded.

Standing up, Morgan walked over to me and placed her hands on either side of my face. The smile she gave me was loving and it even filled her irises. That expression, alone, gave me cause to worry. But it also made me feel safe and secure. Like I really had nothing to worry about.

"Tonight, my dearest Alexandria, you are going to Ascend. And it will be the most powerful, most exhilarating, most astonishing moment of my long life. Including my own Ascension. Forgive me if I believe that it will be the most life-changing experience you and I will ever share. Thank you, Lex, for allowing me to be a part of this. To be a part of *you*."

I couldn't speak. There was a lump in my throat that allowed no words to escape. Holding back tears, I could only nod as I wrapped my arms around her in a tight hold.

As I held her, the cloying scent of a flower seemed to seep out of her skin and clothes. It was a part of her and had been for a long time-though not from before this summer. My mind drifted along this path as I held my beloved teacher and best friend close to me.

As I was letting go, I was able to identify the mystery scent.

Oleander.

It was after nine before the sun set. Morgan and I prepared in the cottage. We both smudged with whichever herbs would help us. Me, being the Ascending, got the full dosage of everything that would cleanse, purify, bless, protect, calm, and focus me.

I had been fasting from that morning, having only a little water to drink all day. It could only help to have an empty stomach when power decided to enter you. I remembered my Wiccaning all too well. The more room I had in my body for the power to fill tonight, the better.

When our preparations were complete, Morgan and I pulled the hoods of our cloaks over our heads and headed out to the circle. Tonight was not a night for besoms and athames, wands and chalices, or even candles and elements. Nothing was needed to call on the power if one had earned it. It would come no matter what was being done.

The rain beat down on us with every step. We let it. It was washing away who I was. Preparing me for who I was to become. With every drop, it stole away with my memories, my past. Each rush of wind tore away the present. I was left with one solid path: the future. This was what I was preparing for. A future. My future.

I sensed the circle long before we reached its rocky borders. Somehow, even with the light of the full moon blocked by the roiling storm clouds, the stones glowed with their own luminescence. The energy of spells long cast were harbored in these stones. Protecting them and aiding others.

Without a moment's pause, I stepped over the low rock wall and made my way to the center. Morgan headed north, to the position of Spirit. Just as I'd seen in my vision. A vision I wasn't so sure I wanted to live through. But I was Ascending, one way or the other.

As I stood on the spot where Mary Sullivan was burned centuries ago, I took a deep breath before grounding and centering myself. Facing north, I raised my head to the sky and just let the rain beat down on me for a moment longer. With another preparatory breath, I raised my hands from my sides, palms up. Then I opened my mouth and a language all my own rolled off of my tongue.

My Ascension had begun.

It could have been seconds. Minutes. Hours or days. I'd not have noticed. The rain washed away all that I was. The wind stole all that I am. The circle held me in the ultimate in-between. Day and night. Today and tomorrow. Shadow and light. In this world and the spirit one.

With each flash of the lightning, I saw a face. Someone I knew. Someone I never met. All of whom had stories that were stitched into my heart, written on my soul. And in each roll of thunder I heard the voices. Blessed. Damned. Angel. Demon. Human. Beast. Dead. Alive. Mental. Physical. There was no way to tell.

Still I chanted away. Calling on the change. The power. The future being forged of liquid fire. A future. My future. A life. My life. A future. My future. A life. My life. *My power!*

In that one, everlasting moment, the world

seemed to halt. My heartbeat slowed. My eyes were frozen wide and I could not force out the next word in my mantra. Everything in the entire universe was focused on one thing alone.

The light coalesced deep in the clouds. Black, roiling masses stopped moving as a ball of gold gathered itself for this one moment. Each second was broken down into milliseconds as the ball of light expanded beyond any brightness I had ever seen. Growing slowly, my eyes took in every single movement of the electric mass.

The ball of light exploded! Lightning flashed across my vision and I was blinded. With an instinctive knowledge, I knew the bolt's destination. I did not move.

I was hit with a red-hot steel beam. Piercing me straight through, I felt speared as I was knocked to the ground. Inside of me, the fire had come alive, remaking me; re-forging me. I was iron turned to steel. Sand transformed into glass. A rock broken away to reveal a diamond. Within my body, the fire burned away every last shred of the person that I was, leaving in its wake the person I was always meant to be.

And the thunder rolled.

Chapter Seventeen

GOODBYE

The feeling of being torn apart and put back together was killing me. It was as bad as Mary Sullivan's burning. I felt every lick of fire running through my veins. Something felt wrong. This power, this drug, it filled me up to the brim, and I burst apart at the seams because of it. My Wiccaning hadn't felt like this, and this was only supposed to be an extension of that.

Or so I thought.

It felt like hours but my body knew that it lasted only a minute. As soon as it hit 12:01, the fire was gone. It felt as if my entire body was remade. The burn embroiled upon my chest vanished, as if it had never existed. I couldn't even feel a bruise. My skin felt like silk-all over, not just where I was struck. The scent coming off my skin was pure ivy. Just like Morgan's was pure oleander this afternoon.

Another minute passed before I could open my eyes. I breathed out of my mouth and, contrary to the heat of the transformation, my breath was cold. Even against my lips. *I* was cold-as if I'd been dunked in ice water, or pulled out of the lake.

Another minute passed while I adjusted to my new senses. There were still voices in the thunder. Still faces in the lightning. Yet, I could hear beyond the voices. The woods were alive with the sounds of foliage being pelted by the rain. All around me, the guardian circle hummed and pulsed with its very own heartbeat. My heartbeat.

There was something else. Morgan. Her steps came closer and I could hear even her flurried heartbeat. It was too fast. Her pace was too slow, and her breathing was quick and shallow. Something was wrong. Her heart was flying. Just like it would if it were about to fail.

The panic forced me to my feet. If I had been the me I was only five minutes ago, I'd have stumbled, but I was different now. I wouldn't call it supernatural-I wasn't faster or stronger than before-but I was more aware of how my body moved and what it could and could not do. As I stood in the center of the circle, Morgan stepped into the center with me.

Morgan stepped into the place where she was born. She came here to die.

"No," I whispered. "Not here. Not now. I need you!"

Morgan smiled that hateful, knowing smile at me and her icy eyes were full of understanding and guilt. Guilt for worrying me, misleading me, deceiving me, and guilt for teaching me. I could read it as easily in her eyes as if I were inside her mind.

Anger ignited inside me. Anger and betrayal. How could she bring me this far, only to abandon me now? How *dare* she *choose* to leave me? What was happening to her now was not natural; she'd chosen this end.

"No, Lex. You don't need me anymore. You never needed me to begin with."

"That is not true," I snarled through my teeth. Tears flooded my vision and I blinked them away angrily. I needed to see her face. To confront her.

"It *is* true, Lex. You've never needed anyone. You're a strong and independent young woman. Truth be known, I needed you more than you could ever need me. You helped me to regain my balance." There were tears in her eyes, too, and I couldn't stop the gasping sob that escaped my throat.

"But I do need you," I said through my tears.

Morgan grabbed my wrists and placed my hands and hers over top of my heart-where the lightning had struck. "If you ever really need me, Alexandria, here is where I'll be."

"But I want you *here*. In *this* world; with me."

"It's too late, Alexandria. This moment has been due for too long. I'm just glad I was able to see you Ascend. It truly was one of the most memorable moments of my life."

"Don't do this," I begged again. To no avail. She was right, it was too late.

"I love you, Lex. You mean more to me than I could ever express."

Sobbing, I threw myself into her open arms and hugged her as tight as I could. My magick pulsed around me and I wanted so badly to flush her system and make what was killing her disappear. Knowing that, Morgan deflected my attempts; determined to die her way. She still had enough strength for that. The situation only made me cry harder.

"I love you, Morgan. I love you. I love you," I whispered over and over and over again.

As I spoke, her heart beat faster and faster. In my arms, I could feel her becoming weaker and we inched downward to the ground. I cradled her, bending over her head as the rain continued to pour down on us.

This can't be happening. I just Ascended. She cannot be dying!

Morgan lay in the circle with her head in my lap. Each breath became harder and harder for her to catch. The effects of the toxin were taking too great a toll on her heart. It spread through her body as the blood rushed at speeds it was very much unused to. For each moment she lay there, she was slipping away from me. Her life was being washed away just as much as mine had been.

Time almost got lost to me, except that I was

still so very aware of my surroundings. After a while, Morgan's heart went from speeding to slowing dramatically. I bit my lip as the seconds ticked by and her heart moved at a sluggish pace until her pulse was well below normal. Then it happened.

I knew the exact second when Morgan took her last breath. At 12:13, a flash of lightning lit up the sky and I got one last clear view of my mentor's face.

Morgan looked peaceful. Willing. Accepting. And relieved. She truly wanted to die.

Her last breath disappeared in the rolling thunder and her eyes closed in her final moment. All the tension faded away from her body as it settled to the ground.

I was alone.

All alone.

It was hours before I could move. Hours before I could think. My mind had wrapped me in the secure bandages of shock-induced numbness that it reserved for the most traumatic moments of anyone's life. This was mine. And that numbness was absolutely what I needed. Without it, I could not function.

The lightning and thunder stopped at about 2:30. At 3 in the morning, the clouds drifted far enough away to allow the full moon to re-enter my world. To guide me home, no doubt.

Awoken from my stupor, I knew I had to get back. I had to deal with this. I had to get Morgan home. That's all I thought about as me and my magick moved in a trance.

Morgan's body was lifted off of me and her cloak wrapped itself around her, covering her entire being so that I couldn't even see her face. I pushed myself to my feet, locking my knees when they threatened to buckle. My shins and thighs tingled painfully from sitting for so long. Even that much was to be grateful for, seeing as it woke the rest of my body bit by bit. After a minute, I was able to regain some form of control over my muscles.

By the light of the full moon, I took Morgan home. She floated ahead of me and I felt like I was in a funeral procession. The situation was nothing short of mournful as I continued through the moonlit woods. My cloak dragged the ground and I could hear every brush of wet grass, leaves, ferns, and sticks.

In that brilliant, numb paradise, I was able to wonder at how unlucky Morgan's family seemed to be when it came to water. For children born of its endless emotions, too many generations had been kissed last by their own element. At the same time, part of me thought that would be the best way to go: carried away by your very own element.

Except, in my case, I had tasted enough fire in my lifetime. Being cremated after the fact was one thing. To be licked alive by hungry flames...

The time it took to return did not seem long enough. Too soon I would have to face what happened. Too soon my numb shell would be broken apart like glass. Too soon I would have to make the phone calls. And too soon I would have to admit that she was really gone.

Morgan was gone.

I loved her and she left me.

Morgan is gone.

Chapter Eighteen

PROMISE

Morgan's body was lying on the bed and I was trying to work up the energy to do something. I had felt so drained the moment she was settled. It was coming back to me, the pain and guilt. A hole seemed to have opened in my stomach and everything but the sorrow was trapped inside.

I couldn't even figure out *why* she had done it. And the how of it…

My feelings of betrayal and confusion began to seep to the surface. One was kindling. The other a match. Both ignited an angry fire inside of me and my disbelief just added fuel to the flames.

Why? How? The two questions I would never let go of for as long as I lived.

Turning away from the bedroom, I gained

the focus necessary to make the phone calls. My anger had done that much for me, at least. I could get something productive done.

As I made to plug in the house phone, however, I made an all too important discovery.

Lying open on the large wooden table was Morgan's Book of Shadows. My stomach plummeted as soon as I saw the picture of an all-too-familiar plant drawn neatly onto the page. A plant that grew only in Mediterranean-like climates. A plant that couldn't naturally stand the cooler temperatures this far north. A plant that Morgan hadn't planted in her garden until the day after my thirteenth birthday.

A plant I was told to avoid.

A plant that was pure toxin.

A plant whose scent would haunt me forever.

Oleander.

The oleander was described in neat, concise paragraphs that detailed all that Morgan had been able to learn of the plant; including its various effects on the human body. A number of symptoms Morgan could have easily hidden from me if her exposure was as long as I suspected. Her cardiac failure had been so sudden that, had she had prolonged exposure, she must have at least tripled the dose.

I could not believe it. I couldn't understand why she had decided to kill herself. And why use oleander? It made no sense.

Feeling my anger boiling inside of me, I slammed the book shut and put it back where she kept it–protected from other people. Then I turned and shoved the cord for the phone into the jack and picked up the receiver before calling 9-1-1.

"9-1-1. Please state the nature of your emergency."

In a hard, empty voice I answered, "I want to report a suicide at the house on Old Grove Road." I didn't even wait for her to ask me to stay on the line. I hung up the phone. There was only one house down this road. They couldn't not know.

It took me another minute before I could gather together the courage to make the next phone call. So many times, I talked myself out of doing it. Of just waiting until the usual time tomorrow. But I had made a promise, and Anne had a right to know.

With shaking fingers, I dialed the next

phone number. It rang four times before going to an answering machine. I hung up and redialed. That wasn't something to be left on an answering machine. The phone picked up on the first ring.

"Alex!" Nathan gasped into the phone. He sounded like he'd just woken up from a nightmare.

Suddenly, I could see him standing in a dark room. Their living room, probably, with the cordless phone in his hand. Nathan stood in pajama bottoms without a shirt on. A shiny cover of sweat coated his bare chest and his eyes were wild. As if he'd seen something he never wanted to see again.

"Yes. It's me. You were right." I couldn't force out another word and I began to sob right then.

"I'm coming over," he said into the phone. I nodded before I realized that he couldn't see me like I could see him.

"Have your mom drive you."

"We're coming."

I hung up once more and the vision of Nathan disappeared with his voice.

At that moment, something happened. I leapt to my feet and returned to Morgan's room where all of the cats had gathered. Lying right by her head, I found the body of her Familiar. He had shed his own life with hers. As if this situation couldn't be any more heartbreaking.

As I walked into the room, my own Familiar turned to stare at me with glowing green eyes. She didn't move anything but her head and eyes. Even her tail stayed still on the bedding as she lay beside Morgan's legs. The ash and tabby cat were on either side of her arms above her elbows. And by her knees, across from my Familiar, was the last cat.

Stifling a sob, I turned from the room and felt the vehicles turning onto Old Grove Road. The wind rushed through the canopies of the mighty oaks; the silent giants were in protest against the people now invading their endless corridor. I couldn't blame them. I didn't want them here any more than the oaks did.

Before they could arrive, I lit the fire to allow more light. Various candles around the room also sprang to life as I made my way to the door. I had to do something before they paraded themselves in here. It wouldn't be right to have them trampling all over the place.

Leaving the door open, I moved out to the gate and waited for the vehicles to come to a stop. There was a cop car and an ambulance. Both without the lights or sirens. They didn't pull out all the stops unless they were sure someone could be saved. From my phone call, they knew that it didn't call for the whole ordeal.

As they exited their vehicles, I opened the garden gate and stepped out to meet them. "Can you try to watch the line, please? And stay on the path?" I asked in a choked voice as the EMS guys removed a gurney from the back.

The cops were as nervous as the kids I went to school with. They were jumpy just being this close to the witch's house. And they would probably start sweating once inside the gate. Pathetic. Idiots with guns they could handle. An old woman and magick was too much for them.

"Gary, go check inside the house. I'll get the girl's statement," one officer said to the other.

"Watch the cats. They know that she's gone. Leave the dead one. I'll take care of him as soon as you're all gone," I murmured, stunning the officers even further. The two men with the gurney paused in mid-step to look at me in surprise, then the one shook his head and they stepped through the gate.

With the two EMS boys leading the way, Gary followed them into the house. I was gratified to see that they all took special care to step over the salt line. Even the cop.

Turning back to the other officer, I made sure to keep my numb shell. Before he could ask me a thing, however, his partner's voice rang through the air. "Hey, Rob, you should get in here!"

Both Rob and I turned toward the opening. "Stay here," the cop muttered before taking off in the direction of the house. Leaning back against the gate, I closed my eyes and saw the whole thing.

"I thought the kid said this was a suicide?" Gary muttered as Rob made his way to the bedroom.

"That's what the call came in as."

"Well, judging by how stiff this body is, she's been dead for a couple of hours. So why is she still soaked to the skin?" one of the ambulance guys remarked.

"The body was moved?" Rob asked in apparent confusion.

Both of the EMS guys nodded their heads with expressions that suggested it were obvious. Rob sighed and ran a hand over his face.

"Is that it?"

"No. Look how she's bound up in her cloak. Would a-what?-seventy-pound kid be able to stage her like that, you think?"

Gary and Rob both raised their eyebrows. "You forget who's lying on that bed there? Or who that kid is? I wouldn't put anything past the freaky shit that happens here. Look at that cat, for crying out loud. He's warm *and* dead."

"Rob, we may not be detectives, but Charlie and I have seen enough crime scenes in our day. This ... this looks pretty staged. You might want to call in the big boys before we go any further."

"C'mon guys. Let's just get the kid's statement. We'll go from there if we have to. And if it makes you feel better, Gary call the boss. Tell him we want a camera."

I'd had enough. Anger flared inside of me at what they were even suggesting. Before I could even *think* to move, I was suddenly standing in the doorway of Morgan's bedroom. I was burning with fury and didn't take the time to examine the sudden transition.

"We were outside when she died. And, from the mouth of a *seventy-five-pound* girl, I can say that it took a while to get her back in here. Calling you guys wasn't exactly on the list of things I could deal with right after watching a loved one die."

All four men jumped and turned to me. At the same time, I felt Anne and Nathan getting closer to the house. I had only a few more minutes alone with these idiots. Then they would be Anne's problem.

"You said this was a suicide. Why didn't you call us right away?" demanded Charlie.

"It is a suicide. Oleander poisoning. I didn't know until it was too late. By then all I could do was hold her as her life slipped away. There was nothing *I* could do to stop it; there was no way in hell any of you would have been able to accomplish a different outcome." My voice was as icy as the lake in the dead of winter. My eyes were blazing blue crystals. They had no right.

Anne pulled up into the driveway, where Nathan sprang out of the car before it was even in park. I whipped around, away from the cops, and went to meet him at the front door.

My promise was kept. Now I wanted to go home.

Chapter Nineteen

ADMISSION

I was more than a little surprised when Nathan strode right up to me and gave me a hug the second he saw me standing outside of the house. After all I'd been through, that was just another shock to vibrate through my all-too-aware system. Like he'd done earlier, I patted him awkwardly on the back until he let go.

"Are you okay?" he demanded, still holding my shoulders, backed away to arm's length so he could see my face. My expression was enough to answer. "I'm so sorry, Lex. I … I didn't want to be right. I know how much she meant to you."

And just like that, my anger flared up. With everything that had happened–Morgan's suicide, the cops, the EMS guys, Nathan, and even Anne approaching from behind–I had begun to see red. The last words were the match on the gasoline.

"How could you know, Nathan?" I hissed between my teeth.

His hands dropped and he stepped farther away as he took in my volatile expression. Anne stopped where she was and stared at me with wide eyes. I was too angry to care.

"How could you *possibly* know *anything* about how I'm feeling right now? Did you spend every day for four years at her side?" I yelled, pushing at his chest. "Did you learn the name of every plant in this garden or see things happen *you* couldn't explain?" I shoved him again with each question. "Have you *ever*, for even a *moment*, stepped foot over that salt line just to *talk* to her? No. You didn't. You were too afraid of her! Too scared to make the effort!"

I was crying so hard that everything was blurry. I could feel him ahead of me and that helped me to direct my shoving. He did nothing to stop me. Nathan let me push him and Anne was too stunned to stop the onslaught. Finally, Nathan pushed forward and wrapped his arms around me again. I rebelled so hard that I was pounding and shoving at his chest. In the end, it was my words that made him let go of me.

"You have *no* idea what she meant to me. You have no idea how much I *love* her. She should have been *my* grandmother, not *yours*!" I screamed at him.

The reaction to that was immediate. Anne was so pissed that she drew on every scrap of magick still in her to shoot something painful at me. But I was more aware. And much more powerful–she had never Ascended. I blocked the assault without even turning my head to look at her.

Nathan's mouth dropped and his arms loosened enough to where I could shove him away. In that moment, I lost it all. My strength. My composure. My wits. Even my Ryder Pride. My knees buckled and I collapsed to the ground right there. Tears ran unheeded down my face as violent sobs ripped through me. Tremors shot through me and I couldn't remember feeling so cold in my life.

The last thing I remembered was Nathan kneeling beside me, wrapping his jacket around me and cradling my rocking body against him.

Through a tunnel, I heard Anne's voice announce that she was calling my parents. Even my mind couldn't object as I barely registered the experience.

Leaning my head against Nathan's shoulder, darkness crept in to salve over the pain. I succumbed to the shock with no feeling whatsoever.

My senses were well aware of my dad sitting in the chair by my desk. His emotions were in a roil. Confusion. Hurt. Disbelief. Anger. Worry. And pride. Everything I would have expected when he learned of Morgan's suicide. All of which I expected him to feel when he realized one more horrible thing had happened to me in Cedar Creek.

I was still in such a screwed-up state of mind, I didn't care.

"I'm not okay," I murmured into the silent room.

My dad stiffened in the chair, his apprehension coating the room as his eyes locked on the back of my head. With stiff movements of my own, I rolled onto my back to face him. He tried to keep his emotions out of his eyes when they met mine, but I still knew. I would always know. I would not always care.

"Why didn't you call us?" he asked in a low tone.

I shrugged. "There was nothing you could do."

"We would have been there for you."

An almost bitter laugh escaped me before I said, "There's nothing you can do for me."

"Don't say that, Lex. I'm your father; there's always something I can do for you."

I shook my head. "We both know that isn't true. Not anymore."

"Lex..."

I burrowed my head beneath the blanket, wishing with all my heart that he would go away. If he didn't want me to hurt his feelings, he had the obligation to walk away as soon as possible. Because I was far too apathetic to care what I said anymore.

After a minute, he sighed, "When this situation is worked out, we are going to have a long family talk."

"I don't think we should wait," I said as I sat

up in the bed. "Let me take a shower and you, me, and Mom can talk."

My dad's eyes narrowed as he looked at me. Probably seeing if I would make a run for it. I had to admit, at that point, my stare down was more effective, seeing as I was still shell-shocked at having my best friend kill herself right before my eyes.

"We'll be in the parlor," he said before rising to his feet and marching out of the room.

After a hot shower that seemed to put some burn back in my frozen corpse, I dressed and prepared to face my parents. There was a bad feeling in my stomach that I couldn't quite place. But it was time to come clean. With Morgan's death, there were a lot of questions I had yet to answer. Who deserved answers more than my parents?

Just as my dad said, they were waiting for me in the parlor. They were huddled together on a sofa, whispering over the things I had experienced. Morgan's name came up too often for my liking. Without even looking at them, I went to the piano and placed my hands on the keys.

A song I had heard so long ago was produced from both my fingers and my throat. My mother,

I knew, would recognize the piano strokes. The words, however, were mine alone, since I was one of the few living people to know the lullaby in its entirety.

As I finished, I was choking back tears. Slowly, I turned around on the bench to face the couch. My parents' faces were set in utter disbelief. Taking a deep breath, I met their eyes and began to explain.

"Alyssa Rice loved that lullaby. She often made her best friend, Victoria, sing it to her while she played. Victoria's mother sang it to her every night. I imagine, she sang it to her daughter every night before they were separated. Victoria was Morgan's mother. She was also the murderer of Alyssa Rice."

My mother was the first to break out of her stunned silence. "My God, Lex. How do you know that?"

"You might want to relax a little, Mom. This is going to be a *long* story."

Chapter Twenty

FACING FACTS

"This is impossible," my dad grumbled once I'd finished my tale. I had to hand it to him, he had stayed still and silent all through the debriefing. "You must have hit your head or something, Lex. There's just no way all of that is even possible."

Already there was a large chasm forming between us. Now, it had grown to canyon-like proportions. This wasn't exactly something I was expecting. Or anything I was close to prepared for.

"Well, it's real, Dad," I ended up snapping, causing him to shoot a scathing glare my way. I almost felt like he'd slapped me with his eyes. My father never glared at me before and it was hard to take.

"Lex, why didn't you tell us any of this?"

I sighed at my mother's question and closed my eyes in order to focus. "I didn't want you to interfere," I forced out, still not looking at them. "You both would have freaked out that I was hanging out with a witch. You, at least, would have tried to fill up my time so that I couldn't go to see her. Dad, you would have just banned me from seeing her. Neither would have helped either of you, since I'd have gone anyway, but it was best not to push the limits at the time."

"I'm sorry, Lex, but this isn't something I can believe without proof. I know you think you are capable of doing all these things, but what you're describing just isn't possible," my mom tried to assure me.

At times like this I was torn. Morgan's philosophy worked the best: let them believe what they like, but don't become their show pony. However, these were my parents. They had a right to know. They'd never believe me otherwise.

Instead of answering, I split myself in two and was a little surprised at how easy it was to control the different bodies. Another thing to chalk up to my Ascension. The other me came in from the hallway-so as to scare my parents less-and walked right up to my mother. It was harder for them to deny when two Alexandria Ryders stood before them.

"Oh my God," my dad muttered and eased himself back down onto the sofa beside my mother. An arrow shot through my heart when he wrapped his arms around my mother and they both looked frightened.

Holding my tears in check, I let the astral fade. "Now you see why I didn't tell you? You can't accept what I am." The words came out harsher than what I'd intended. "But there's someone who does accept me. Magick and all." Before I knew it, I was on my feet and heading for the front door.

"Alexandria," my dad called. I didn't bother to look back as he followed me.

I knew it surprised him when I yanked open the front door and said, "Hello, Matt." My dad stopped in his tracks to look past me at my surprised boyfriend.

After a second, Matt shook off the surprise and tried to act like it wasn't awkward standing in the open doorway with me looking irritated and upset while my father glowered at me.

"Hey. I just heard. How are you feeling?" I had to hand it to him, he brought things back around to the most important thing at that moment.

Before I could answer, Matt wrapped his arms around me in a tight embrace. For a minute, I couldn't move. It was the touching, I realized. I didn't want him to touch me. None of them should have been touching me. Yet, this was my boyfriend and he was worried. I hugged him back and tried to pretend that my whole universe hadn't turned into a living hell overnight.

After a few minutes, my dad cleared his throat to get our attention. I wiped at my leaking eyes as I turned to face him. At the same time, Matt's fingers laced together with mine. Again, I had to fight the feeling that this was strange and unwanted.

"Matt, maybe you should go home. Alexandria, her mother, and I are in the middle of a discussion."

"Dad, he already knows. Matt doesn't care that I'm a witch." That made him stop and think. "But he's right. Let's take this into the parlor,"

I suggested to my boyfriend. Matt nodded and stepped into the house. Without moving, I glanced at the heavy wooden door and it swung shut of its own accord.

My dad winced. Matt didn't even blink an eye. The difference between them was nigh comical. If this was a day for laughing, that might have been one of those moments that I snickered behind my hand. As it was, my face was empty and expressionless as I towed Matt past my father and into the parlor.

Once there, I turned to Matt and asked in an apathetic tone, "Can you please tell my parents what I'm really like? They're having trouble believing me."

In retrospect, it might not have been very nice to put him on the spot like that. At the same time, this had to get done. And soon. My stomach was still telling me that something bad was about to happen and I needed my parents to know the truth about me *from me*. Matt was, more or less, corroboration.

Matt looked stunned for a minute before meeting my eyes in a meaningful way. He didn't know what he was supposed to say. With a sigh,

I suggested, "Tell them about the movies and the woods. Please?"

Nodding, Matt turned to address my mother– the parent who loved that he was my boyfriend and had always supported us. "When I asked Lex out the first time, we went to the movies. As we were walking to our seats, people were staring and whispering. I could tell that she was uncomfortable, but she just raised her chin even higher and ignored them." Matt smiled at me and I forced myself to smile back. It felt unnatural to turn my lips into anything but a grimace. "After we sat down, someone yelled 'witch' and threw half a cup of soda at her. Somehow ... Lex blocked it. It was like the cup hit an invisible wall and fell to the floor. She was ready to leave after that, since everyone was staring and knew what she could do, but I asked her to stay and watch the movie.

"Then, on one of our walks through the woods, I accidentally tripped us. We both fell to the ground and laid there a moment, just staring up into the treetops. That was when Lex decided that she wanted to test how well I could deal with her magick.

"I'm not sure *what* she did or *how* she did it,

but suddenly everything was changing. It went from summer to fall, through winter and spring, and circled back around. It was the most *amazing* thing I've ever seen in my life."

'Thank you,' I mouthed to him and he smiled at me before squeezing my fingers.

Sighing, I turned to face my mother. "I'm not bad. Being a witch doesn't make me evil. I only want the best for people. Which is why Morgan's suicide pisses me off so much. She shouldn't have done that," I added through my teeth as I attempted to blink away angry and sad tears.

Once more, I felt Matt's arms wrap around me and he began murmuring reassurances into my hair. I wasn't sure why, but my parents chose not to interfere. Something I was both grateful for and resentful of.

"I'm so sorry, Lex. I know how much she meant to you," Matt murmured.

As soon as he said that, my eyes snapped open and I leapt back away from him. Memories seeped into my head along with a pang of guilt. My mouth hung open in horror as I looked between my father, mother, and boyfriend.

Feeling panicked, I blurted, "Oh Goddess! I

have to find Nathan!"

Without another word, I turned on my heel and dashed out the front door. Nothing else mattered but that I talk to the only person who'd stuck by me through thick and thin. The person whose family history was revealed last night through my own careless slip.

I looked ahead to find him first. He was at home. His mother and twin were talking in low, intense voices, while Nathan hovered just outside of the room, shamelessly eavesdropping as they whispered and hissed over the demise of their mother. Thanks to me, the cat was out of the bag. Now, it sounded as if they were figuring out a way to do damage control with Nathan. By the way he looked in that vision, they wouldn't have much luck in keeping him quiet.

I needed to get to him. To explain. To control this damage myself, before the twins made anything worse.

Once more, before I could even think about it, I found myself standing just outside their front door. Instead of knocking and alerting the unaware sisters to my presence, I closed my eyes and sent a mental message to my friend.

I'm sorry, Nathan. I understand if you don't want to talk to me, but I'm outside if you do.

With a sigh, I turned from the door and had just sat down on the porch steps when the front door opened behind me. Whipping around, I found him staring at me with a stunned expression on his face. After a minute of staring at me, Nathan came outside and closed the door. Silently, he sat beside me and stared out at the road for a while.

I had no words. Despite all of the apologizing and explanations that I owed him, I couldn't even form the words in my own head. We sat there in silence for about three minutes. Then we glanced at each other at the same time.

I broke.

Tears flooded my eyes and I gasped a sob. "I miss her so much!" As soon as the words were out of my mouth, I threw my arms around Nathan's neck and clung to him. This time there was nothing awkward about our embrace as he hugged me back.

Somehow, I knew that this was right. Nathan

and I had shared Morgan. Only the two of us could share the pain over her loss. No one else could even imagine.

Chapter Twenty One

COMFORTING

A full hour passed where Nathan and I sat on his front porch holding each other. I didn't even budge when I felt Matt appear across the street and watch us for at least five minutes. I was so lost in my own consuming misery that what he thought of that situation did not matter. At all.

I clung to Nathan for selfish reasons. The types of reasons you don't admit to somebody. Ever. Like the fact that I hung onto him mainly because he was a part of Morgan. A distant part, but of her blood nonetheless. She had loved him as she had loved me. He had even come to know her a little bit. And there was an aura of hers that clung to him. Other than the fact that he was my only other friend and I needed his support more than anyone's, the reason I clung to him so much was because he was all I had left of her.

That meant that no one or nothing else mattered.

Only when I felt Sarah and Anne coming toward the door did I let go of him and attempt to wipe my eyes. When Nathan looked at me, there were a million questions in his eyes and I wanted nothing more than to answer them right then. But our time was running short and I could imagine what would happen as soon as the twins opened that door.

Anne was the first to step out onto the porch and she sighed in relief at seeing Nathan there. Her expression turned to stone the moment she noticed me beside him. Maybe it was my own heartbroken expression that allowed her features to soften as she glanced between the two of us.

Before Anne was able to say anything, her sister came out right behind her and her features twisted into a mask of pure rage and fury upon sighting me. Oddly, I was feeling so weak while sitting there with Nathan, I didn't even have the energy to defend myself from whatever she threw my way.

"How dare you?"

I didn't even look to Fay as I replied, "I'm sorry, Nathan. You shouldn't have found out like that. And it shouldn't have been me to tell you."

At last, it was time to talk. Nathan glanced up at his mother and the elder twin nodded and tried to smile to her son. Standing up, Nathan held out a hand to help me to my feet. With how drained I felt, it didn't even bother me to accept his help.

"We're going for a walk," Nathan informed me; we left the twins standing there. I already knew where we were going, but I was up for a lengthy walk. It would give us a lot of time to talk.

"I'm sorry," I murmured yet again.

"Don't be. At least *someone* told me." There was that feeling of iron below his words. The kind that suggested he was holding someone accountable, but that someone wasn't me.

"I'd say not to blame your mom, but it is their fault. Hers and Faylin's. Too damn weak to admit that Morgan was their mother." I said the words with only minimal heat. I was still too dazed to manage a full-blown outrageous fury.

"Faylin?"

"Sarah's real name. Freyja, Fiona, and Faylin. Those were Morgan's daughters. Your mom was once Fiona," I replied in a calm voice. It felt right, telling Nathan about his family. I was being honest with everyone else. Why not him?

"Weird names," he muttered as he walked with his hands shoved in his jeans pockets.

"Weird mother," I was able to reply with the tiniest smile. That made Nathan glance at me with a studying look. Like he was seeing if I was upset again.

"What happened to Freyja?"

That made me look away. I didn't want to tell him, but it would be good for Nathan to have a secret to hold over the twins' heads. At least, I thought so.

"Your mother and aunt don't know this, but Freyja died on their eighteenth birthday. Suicide. At the lake," I whispered. Only afterward did I think it was a bad idea, seeing as Nathan stopped in his tracks with his mouth agape.

After a minute, he shook his head a little and muttered, "I'm never swimming there again."

"I'm sorry, Nathan. If you don't want me to

tell…"

"No. Lex, I want to know. Everything that you know. At least you know the truth. I'm just sorry that I never took the time to learn."

I nodded and we walked a few steps before I whispered, "Me, too." Then I sighed and continued telling him about the things I had learned from both Morgan and his own mother. Then I did the unthinkable for the second time that day: I told him about Alyssa and Victoria. If I was sharing his family history, the least I could do was tell him all that I knew.

Nathan and I walked all the way down to Old Grove Road before his mom's car passed us. They were heading to the house, too. Which meant now it was my turn to ask questions.

"Nathan? What happened after I passed out last night?"

"Well, my mom went in and called your parents. I stayed outside with you…" His voice trailed off as if he thought it would weird me out if he said he was holding me. "Then your parents showed up. At first your dad freaked because he thought something had happened to you. My mom pulled your parents off to the side and explained that Morgan had committed suicide, and you had lost it when we got there. While that was happening, I took you to your car and got you settled in the backseat."

I nodded. "After my parents took me home?"

Nathan sighed and said, "They brought in detectives, Lex. They said it was standard procedure-in order to rule out homicide-but that the cops who responded hadn't followed it because they were sure you were right on it being a suicide. I guess they got a massive ass chewing or something when they reported back. Right now, the house is taped off and everything. But they'll be glad to see you because they didn't get your statement last night. Another thing those cops got in trouble over."

I snorted. "Good luck getting the truth from me now. They didn't when I found Alyssa and they'll get nothing from me now. I just have to go back to make sure they didn't do anything with her cat."

"Oh, they didn't. Mom took him out into the garden and buried him. Then she performed some little ritual for him or something. I'm not sure."

"So then why are we going back? It's not like the cops will let us in the house."

"We're not going to the house. Mom wants to talk to you at the lake. She said you had to pass by in order to see what was going on, but it wasn't safe to talk to anyone there. Lex, I can't believe this. They're under the impression that you had something to do with her death."

I wasn't surprised. "They're idiots." I released a sigh. Then I found myself whispering, "Why'd she do it? Why suicide? And why oleander? It's not a quick, painless death. And her heart was beating *so fast*." Tears filled my eyes and I closed my lids against their escape.

While we were walking, Nathan wrapped an arm around my shoulders and I felt myself wrap an arm around his side. It was right that we had each other. Fiona and Faylin had each other and so did Nathan and I. After a while, I was able to let go of him and wipe my eyes again. This was getting to be a very bad habit.

"So, I have to ask, are you going to tell Morgan's other grandchildren?"

"No. Not unless I have to," he amended with a strange nuance. He was hiding something. He didn't want to tell the other kids, but he would for the right reason.

"Good. I don't think you should. Your mother and Fay grew up in a harsh world. Even worse than how I've been. I'd hate for you to suffer through that, too."

Nathan shook his head and a slight, teasing grin alighted on his lips. "Yes, because I am so popular right now."

"That is another question I always meant to ask you: Why stick it out with me for four years? Through all this bullshit, you've always been there. Why?"

Nathan shrugged and refused to make eye contact. Surprisingly, he was able to bury his emotions from me. The latent magick in him wasn't surprising, but the fact that he'd tapped into it was enough to prove his relationship to Morgan.

"Lex, everybody needs a friend. Even you. And ... it's nice being your friend. Even if we don't talk to each other, we still kinda always have each other's backs. With all that crap going on with you and my connection to her, you were the only one I could really count on. We kept each other's secrets."

I forced a smile as I looked up at Nathan. "We've still got each other's backs. That'll never change."

Nathan smiled back at me as he nodded.

Then we stopped talking.

Chapter Twenty Two

STATEMENT

It wasn't a long conversation Anne and I had. She filled me in on the current steps in the investigation, along with the fact that I would have to give my statement to the detectives. Soon.

"They'll never believe me. You know that," I countered.

"We all know it was a suicide, Alexandria. That's all you have to tell them. The sooner you do that, the sooner we can all put this whole ordeal behind us."

I snorted at that. "Put this behind us? What makes you think I'm capable of that? Nothing stays buried around me."

Anne opened her mouth, but I caught Nathan shaking his head out of the corner of my eye. I was surprised when his mother sighed and closed her mouth again. Then Nathan put his hand on my shoulder.

"You're right, Lex. There's no way you are not going to feel this for the rest of your life. That doesn't mean you won't get past it. You know better than anyone how to keep going even when everything is falling apart."

Tears welled up in my eyes and I tried to glare at him through my watery vision. "What makes you think I can this time? She left me, Nathan. Not you, or her daughters. Me. I was the last person to enter into her life, and I'm the one she left behind."

"I don't think, Lex, I *know* you can get through this. You have never let anything stop you. And you're certainly not going to let Morgan be the one thing that does."

Despite the fact that I still wanted to argue with him, a smile pulled at my lips. Wiping the tears from my face, I tried to grimace at him. "Since when did you become so smart?"

He shot me a tiny grin. "I've always been smart. You just didn't take the time to notice."

I rocked sideways and shoved my shoulder

against him before sighing and turning to Anne once more. "What's going to happen now?"

Nothing was more honest than the forlorn expression on her face. "I don't know, Alex. I wish I did."

I gave a nod before turning to look back down Old Grove Road. The commotion half a mile down was enough to cause the trees and plants to sink into themselves, their conscious thoughts no longer making a melody of energy between each other. Everyone was protecting themselves, now that their protector was gone. Now that things were in a vast state of the unknown.

My first instinct was to comfort them. To reach out with my own energy and prod theirs back to life with the promise that I would always be there. Yet, a foreboding existed in me and I dared not make a promise I might not be able to keep. Right now, it was as much my duty to protect myself as it was theirs.

"Lex?" Nathan murmured beside me.

"I think I have to go home now," I muttered back, feeling a sense of urgency I wasn't in the habit of experiencing.

Instead of moving, however, I closed my eyes and cast my vision ahead. Remote viewing was a gift Morgan had had in spades. It was how she always knew what was going on in town or with me. I used to wonder what she did all day, but now I knew. She people-watched, without ever leaving the comforts of her home.

Now, I used the same gift to look into the parlor at my house and found two detectives sitting down with my parents. Polite questions were being asked and coffee was being sipped, but I had no doubt that they were in a stage of stasis. One that would break into full-blown activity once I arrived.

Opening my eyes, I looked to Nathan and didn't even try to hide the panic in my gaze. "They're waiting for me. The detectives."

Instead of saying anything, Nathan's eyes shot to his mother. Silent as her son, Anne nodded once before turning to look at Sarah. That one took more than a few seconds of communication, but Morgan's other daughter eventually nodded.

As soon as she did, Nathan turned to me and said, "We'll give you a ride. It'll be faster than walking."

I almost told him right then that I didn't have to walk. For one, long second, I wanted to show him what my Ascension had done for me. To me. But I didn't want to show Fiona or Faylin. They didn't need to know. So, it became one more secret that was all mine. For now.

"Thank you," I answered before we all headed to Anne's car. As Nathan and I settled ourselves in the backseat, I asked, "Was it bad? When you gave your statement?"

"Not really," he hedged. "They didn't seem inclined to want to believe that Morgan said goodbye to me. It was something they kept going over and over, to see if I would change my story or anything. And they asked me a lot of questions about you."

I nodded. That much, I had expected. After the reaction the cops had to her body being laid out the way it was, I knew this was going to be an uphill battle. With this following on the heels of the Alyssa Rice incident, I had very little hope for how this conversation was going to turn out. At least I had Nathan and Anne with me. Even Sarah. Out of anyone, they knew best what was happening with me. My parents didn't understand my magick, but it could come as no surprise to the descendants of Morgan.

Anne pulled into my driveway and parked behind my dad's car, leaving the detectives room to back out. I kept my eyes trained on the front of the house, and was rewarded with my mother's familiar face appearing in the window to see who was intruding. When I got out of the car, I could almost see the relief set in.

For a moment, I stood staring at the house. How could someplace so familiar seem so formidable? With the detectives sitting in my parlor, making polite small talk with my parents, it felt like stepping foot through that door was akin to walking into a trap.

"Come on, Lex. The sooner this is over with, the better," Nathan muttered beside me.

For him, I tried to smile. Instead, I grimaced a bit before taking a deep breath and heading for the front door. Nathan kept in step beside me while Anne and Sarah followed us. My mom was there, waiting for us, by the time we reached it.

"Hey, Mom," I muttered as we stood staring at one another for a minute. "You sort-of know Nathan and his mom, Anne. This is Sarah, Anne's twin sister."

"It's a pleasure to see you again. Nice to meet you," she murmured to my posse. Then her gaze zeroed in on me, once more. "Lex..."

"I know," I answered before she let me move past her. I went straight to the parlor. No point in drawing it out any further. And maybe Nathan was right; the sooner I clued them into the facts, the sooner I would be done with this whole thing.

"Gentlemen, this is my daughter, Alexandria," my dad said as I entered the room. I think I shocked both detectives when I strode up to them and held out my hand for them to shake.

"Detective Stone," announced the man with the graying brown hair who was skinny as a rail. There was a hard gleam in his eyes that I distrusted in an instant.

"Detective Ross," said the other man. His black hair held less gray and his features made him at least three years his partner's junior. He also had a more filled out frame, suggesting he made regular use of the gym. He seemed no more likely to believe me than his partner.

Both men were even more surprised when Anne, Sarah, and Nathan followed my mom into the room. They almost exchanged a glance, but caught themselves at the last second while the rest of us found surfaces to sit on. Being that they were there to see me, I was sandwiched between my parents on the sofa across from theirs while Nathan took a seat on the piano bench. Behind me to the right, the twins shared the settee.

Once they realized that this was how it was going to be, the two men did exchange a look. They wanted to talk to me alone, I understood. Since I was a minor who wasn't being charged with anything, I had the right to have my parents with me. As long as I was comfortable with it, I couldn't see the harm in Morgan's family being there as well.

"Well, Alexandria, I think you know why we are here," Detective Stone said at last.

I nodded. "You want to know about Morgan's suicide."

Detective Stone's eyebrows rose a little. "Yes, we would like to know about Ms. LeFayette's death."

"What would you like to know?"

Detective Ross pulled out a pad of paper and flipped to a blank page. "What were you doing at

Mrs. LeFayette's house yesterday evening?"

"I was spending the night."

"And what did you do while you were spending the night?" prodded Detective Stone.

Resisting the urge to sigh, I said, "During the early evening, we prepared for a ritual to take place at midnight. For that, I took a cleansing bath. I'm not sure what Morgan was doing at that time."

"What kind of ritual was this?" Detective Ross asked while scribbling away.

"It was an Ascension rite to be performed for me. A pagan ritual associated with witchcraft, if you need a more cut-and-dry description," I added when he paused in his writing.

Both sets of eyes narrowed in on me in an instant. "Were you and Ms. LeFayette active participants in witchcraft?" Detective Stone demanded.

For one moment, I was no longer a thirteen-year-old girl sitting in front of two detectives as they asked about my best friend's suicide. Instead, I was an impertinent nine-year-old who was asking the old woman I had just met if she wanted me to tell the other kids that she was a witch. As I was sitting there, a smile pulled up my lips as I heard her voice say, "*I brook no dishonesty in my house. I would not ask for a lie from your lips.*"

"Yes," I murmured a moment later, the smile still on my lips. "Yes, we were both active in the Craft. We are witches."

"And you were with her last night to perform a ritual pertaining to witchcraft?" Detective Stone repeated.

I nodded. "Yes."

"Let's start at the beginning: what time did you arrive at Ms. LeFayette's home?"

Chapter Twenty Three

CHANGE

At least an hour passed before the detectives left. Each one giving me the promise of returning when they had more questions. A promise it was too unfortunate to doubt.

For the most part, it had been easy to answer their questions. Though I think I surprised them again when I knew everything down to the minute. Yet, when it came to questions such as where she died and how I got her back into her bed on my own, my answers were a little less helpful, and they knew it.

The worst part, however, was how they reacted to Nathan. As they were saying goodbye, it wasn't my imagination that had them looking at Nathan suspiciously, before their eyes trailed back to me. I knew then and there that they thought he was my accomplice. They thought Nathan had helped me move Morgan's body. That was when I realized just how bad this was.

"They don't believe it was a suicide," I announced once the detectives had pulled out of the driveway.

"No, they don't," Sarah said in a hard voice that I didn't understand. "For now, there's nothing else for them to go on. With any luck, this will all blow over in a week."

My eyes met her across the room, and we spoke as if we were the only two there. "You don't think I'm that lucky, do you?"

"No. They'll come back. Several times over several weeks. Maybe months. When they do, call me," she answered. My head tilted to the side and she gave me a wry smile. "I'm a criminal defense attorney. And I know that your mentor committed suicide. I'll be here when you need me."

"Thank you," I muttered, grateful for the offer. The foreboding in my stomach told me that I would have to take her up on it. One day soon.

Following that moment, Sarah, Anne, and

Nathan all left. Which put me back in the awkward position of dealing with my parents. I'd been a bit pleased at their lack of protest when Morgan's family had joined us for the questioning, but I knew better than to think that would be the end of it. Sure enough...

"Alexandria, what was all of that about?" my dad demanded.

I didn't turn away from the window as I sighed, "That was about the detectives believing me to be responsible for Morgan's death. They think I killed her, Dad."

He didn't know what to say to that. None of us did. To everyone who knew me, the idea was so incomprehensible that it rendered us speechless. I wasn't capable of hurting Morgan. I wished I could have said the same for Morgan hurting me.

True to their word, the detectives returned at least once a week for the rest of the summer. They would ask the same questions over and over again, trying to see if my answers would change. When that failed, they tried pressing my buttons, especially about the location of Morgan's death.

On that point, I shut up right quick.

In the meantime, an autopsy was performed on Morgan's body and it was released to her family. What the authorities were unaware of—and I only knew because Nathan told me—was that Sarah had a second autopsy performed on her mother's body. I didn't understand the necessity of it, but Nathan assured me it was to have our bases covered in the event this all went to hell.

After the second autopsy, Sarah allowed Morgan's remains to be cremated. Anne dropped the ashes off to me the day before school was to start. She didn't say anything and I asked nothing from her as she handed over the urn. And while I had every intention of spreading Morgan's ashes in the circle, I found that I couldn't face that yet. So the urn was placed on the small mantel above my bedroom fireplace, and I did my best to avoid looking at it every day.

The day after I gave my first statement, Matt showed up to talk to me. Like we had done many times before, we went on a walk through the woods. Unlike before, we no longer held hands and there were several inches of space between us. Things had changed.

"I warned you," I told him when we'd gone five minutes without speaking.

Instead of playing dumb, he nodded. "Yeah, you did. But that was back when we were still sure you would like me after your ritual. Neither of us were counting on this."

"No. No, we weren't," I sighed. "I do still like you, Matt. Even enough to be your girlfriend. But I'm not whole right now, and I don't think I have it in me to care about you. It's hard enough caring about me."

"I understand, Lex. Really, I do. Right now, what you need is a friend, and I can be that. If we decide to be together in the future, we have that option."

The smile wasn't forced as I turned to hug him. It was a relief, really. I didn't want my first breakup to be messy and complicated, and he had made it the easiest thing I would deal with for the rest of the summer. From that point on, Matt and I were friends. By the end of summer, we were more like siblings, bringing us to the mutual decision that we would never have a recap.

Perhaps the only other easy ordeal was the media stuff. I had a reporter stop by my house once to see if I would give a statement or an interview concerning Morgan's death. I told them I had nothing to say concerning her suicide. True to form, however, they ran with what I told them and the local newspaper said that her death appeared to be a suicide. A fact which irritated the detectives, but without evidence to say otherwise, they couldn't order a retraction. They got to the local TV station before me, however, and it was announced that Morgan's death was under investigation.

After the past few weeks, it was hard to imagine that school could even compare as far as difficulty went. For a while, my parents discussed me staying at home. My mom was even considering quitting her job. Something I was adamant in refusing. Not only was I against being pulled out of school, but I knew how much my mother would hate not working. She was a busy-body who knew the dictionary definition of relax, but couldn't fathom what it meant for her as a person.

Yet, the same kind of foreboding that was

haunting me must have also been lingering around them. I learned about a week before school was to start that my mom agreed to teach the first semester, but that someone else would take over in January. There were other teachers on standby, however, to fill her position if things with me became more determined sooner than I expected. Whatever that meant.

"Lex? Ready for bed? You've got to get up early tomorrow," my mom murmured.

My head snapped up and whipped toward the doorway to the parlor. I hadn't even realized that I'd moved to the piano. Of course, as the last haunting note filled the air, I knew why. It was Victoria's Lullaby I was playing. Over the past few weeks, I had come into the habit of playing it whenever I was thinking about things.

I nodded for a bit before I got up from the bench. "Yeah. I'm ready," I sighed.

The truth of the matter was that I was far from ready to return to school. Between my Ascension and Morgan's suicide, I wasn't sure how I could handle sitting in a classroom and pay attention to things that wouldn't affect my life in any meaningful way. I knew what my life entailed now, and school had very little to offer as far as my future went.

At the same time, I thought it might be a welcome distraction from all of my other problems. I didn't have to be the world's greatest student; I just had to pass. That would have to be enough for my parents, because I wasn't going to waste effort on it when I had far more important matters to deal with.

Pausing in the doorway, I turned to look at my mom. Her eyes were a darker hue, meaning she was worried. She was always worried now. There was nothing I could do to change the way she looked at me.

"I'm not the daughter you thought I would be," I murmured before the thought had formed in my mind.

Her eyes widened in surprise as I gave her my new, dead stare. "No," she said at last, "you are not the daughter I thought you would be. You are more than I had ever hoped for, Alexandria. Don't ever doubt it."

I gave her a nod before I turned toward the stairs. She stopped me with a hand on my shoulder before drawing me into a tight hug. We stood like that for about five minutes before she released me. And it haunted me all night that I might never be around my mother without knowing how afraid she was to be in the same room with me.

Chapter Twenty Four

SHADOW

When I got on the bus the following morning, I was less than surprised to find that most people stopped speaking and watched my progress as I chose a seat near the back. Though it was technically High Schooler territory, I knew that they wouldn't mess with me. No one wanted to anger the witch; especially one that might have committed murder. Of course, the minute Matt got on, he plopped down in the seat beside me and threw an arm around my shoulders like it was no big deal.

"I think this counts as trespassing," he remarked.

My lips curled into a sarcastic grin. "I think this counts as harassment, too, but I won't call the cops if you won't."

"Miss Legal, are we now?" he said as he let his arm fall back to his side.

The smile faded as I took a deep breath. "Have to be with my situation."

His own smile faded as we shared one of those intense moments where he wanted me to read his mind. I did, and it was what I expected. He wanted to know how the situation was going, and I didn't feel like talking about it. A fact he relented on when I cut off the contact and stuck my tongue out at him.

We spent the rest of the bus ride on amicable terms until we pulled up to the school. The sigh that left me came from deep within my lungs, as I expelled every awful feeling I had for the place. If the bus was any indication, I wasn't sure I wanted to know what the rest of the day would be like.

"Are you going to be okay?" Matt asked as we pulled up to the Middle School.

"No. I don't think I'll ever be okay again," I responded.

"I wish I was able to be with you."

I rolled my eyes. "You'll be in the next building over. It's not a crisis."

"If I didn't know Nathan was going to shadow your every step, I would think it was."

My eyes crinkled into a glare as I stuck my tongue out at him once more. Before he could say anything else, however, it was time for me to go. I gave him a half-smile before proceeding to the front exit. I didn't think he was right about Nathan, until I found the lanky teenager waiting for me.

"You've got to be kidding me," I muttered to him as he fell into step beside me. "Did Matt put you up to this?"

"Lex, if there had never been a Matt, I would still be doing this. Though, to be honest, I would have liked to have my seat back," he added in an attempt to get me to smile.

"Sorry, I think he's claimed it for the duration of the semester, at least."

"We'll discuss it."

I rolled my eyes. There was nothing else for it. Matt and Nathan had worked out some form of understanding over the past couple of weeks and had sort of split custody over me. By now, their ways were mysterious in their own right, and I didn't care enough to figure them out.

"Have you guys decided my holiday arrangements as well?" I muttered as we headed inside. Nathan rolled his eyes.

As Matt predicted, Nathan played at being my shadow for the rest of the day. Since we had most of the same classes, it didn't bother me as much. When we sat side by side-me claiming the seat in the back corner, farthest from the door, so that I could see everything-it was in the same companionable silence we had always shared.

The only time he was more than arm's length away from me was in the cafeteria. I had declined any form of food since my appetite wasn't where it should have been. Not that I thought choking down school food would do it any good. I went to find a seat while Nathan waited in the lunch line.

During one of the many moments where he was looking back at me, I locked eyes with him across the room and shook my head. This was getting to be ridiculous, but I couldn't think of a way to make him stop. I wasn't even sure I cared enough to try.

That's when I saw his cousin, Mark, say

something behind him. It only took a second for Nathan to set down the half-filled tray, turn, and swing. Noisy as it was in the cafeteria, I could still hear his fist connecting on Mark's face.

A burst of panic flared through me and I closed my eyes and set my magick free. My first thought was to dismantle the cameras, and the magick followed the electricity back to the recording box where I corrupted the past five minutes of footage. The cameras would be down for the rest of the day, which meant I had time to get my watchdog out of a suspension. I went from sitting at a table to standing beside Nathan in the blink of an eye. Without bothering to pose a question, I grabbed Nathan's arm and we were gone in another blink.

I didn't take him far; we popped up behind the gym, on the grassy field surrounded by the track with goalposts at either end. If I took him too far from school, it'd be difficult to suggest we return to class when the bell sounded. Though I think that was a precaution for me more than it was for him.

"Whoa," he breathed in a voice barely above a whisper as he stumbled forward a few steps.

"Sorry," I muttered when it seemed his blurry vision had dissipated. "I didn't know what else to do, so I thought some time to cool off would help."

"So, you teleported us," he said in the same low tone.

I sighed. "Yeah. I can do that now."

Nathan still didn't turn to look at me, but he nodded in response. "You know we would have been fine, right? I wasn't going to beat him to a pulp or anything. He just needs to learn when to keep his mouth shut."

"Then teach him off of school grounds. You could have been suspended. Or expelled, you know."

"Nah. Mark won't admit that I hit him. He knows the score. And if Mark denies it, no one else will admit to it happening."

"Cameras?" He didn't need to know I'd solved that problem.

"They won't check them unless they have a reason to. Since no one is going to rat me out, they won't bother to see what happened. Mark tripped and caught a table on the way down, or whatever else he wants to tell the teachers. It had nothing to do with me."

My head pulled back a little. "You've put a lot of thought into this," I grumbled.

Nathan turned to me then, a sly smirk on his lips and wicked sparkle in his dark green eyes. "This isn't the first time Mark has needed a lesson in keeping his mouth shut. On school grounds or otherwise." Then the smile faded as he studied me. "Though I do wonder what's going to happen when everyone talks about our disappearing act."

An exasperated sigh pushed itself out of me as I dropped to the ground. Nathan took a seat beside me and waited for my answer.

"I killed the cameras. No one will see that you hit Mark. And no one will see me performing magick. We're covered on that. As far as what anyone says: who's going to believe them?"

For a moment, Nathan stared at me. I knew why. We were both thinking it. The fact that I was a witch and being investigated for murder changed things. At this point, we were in Salem. There was very little the authorities wouldn't believe when it came to me.

Almost as quiet as a whisper, Nathan then

asked me, "What else can you do?"

I almost smiled as I thought back over the past few months. Over what Matt had done to my magick. How instinctive and natural it all felt. Then what my Ascension had done to me. The raw power that flowed through my veins, sometimes making everyday tasks feel like mundane chores. Even walking from room to room was nothing compared to the quick blink of appearing and disappearing.

Lying back on the grass, I stared up at the cerulean sky as I answered, "Everything. I can do everything, Nathan."

Chapter Twenty Five

ROUTINE

During the ride home, Nathan allowed Matt to sit beside me, but only because Matt was one of the first ones off. As soon he neared the door, Nathan hopped from Mark's seat into mine. The grin that spread across his face was infectious and I almost laughed. That urge faded when we stopped at his house and his brother got off.

"What are you doing?" I demanded as we pulled away.

Nathan shrugged. "Think your mom will be mad if I get off at your house without asking for permission?"

"Does it matter?" I scoffed. "Will you get off at the next stop if I say 'yes, she would'?"

His grin was unapologetic. "Nope."

Rolling my eyes, I turned to stare out the window. We didn't talk again until the bus pulled up in front of my house. The driver didn't seem at all surprised when Nathan followed me up the narrow aisle and got off the bus with me.

My mom wasn't home yet when we walked in, so I threw my bag under the stairs and headed for the kitchen. Behind me, I could hear Nathan follow suit. As I went about making an afternoon snack for us, he leaned against the island and tried not to look as out of place as I know he felt.

"I don't need a babysitter, you know."

It surprised me a little when his eyes flashed with hurt before he said, "I know."

My eyebrows rose. "Then why have you spent all day acting like my bodyguard?"

"Sorry, I thought I was acting like your friend."

That forced a snort from me. "Nathan, you punched your cousin today. Because he has a big mouth and he happened to say something about me. That was you being a friend to me?"

"Yes."

I laughed despite myself. "You know, my other friends don't hover around me."

There was no amusement in his expression and I could feel the beginning churn of a storm cloud before he shoved his emotions into that damnable bottle of his. I saw it the moment he decided not to respond to that. The exact second he was certain that saying it wasn't worth the argument that would follow.

He was right. By his silence, I knew he was about to bring up Morgan. Either how she was dead and hovering was all she was capable of, or how if she had protected me a little more, I wouldn't be in the mess I was in now. It wasn't an argument either of us wanted to have, so I let it go, too.

Instead, I turned toward the fridge and asked, "What would you like to drink? I've got water and a few fruit juices. We're not a soda household, I'm afraid."

He forced a smile the same way I forced a light tone: with a lot of effort and minimal success. "Neither is mine. Water, please."

I nodded once before tossing a bottle at him before returning to my task. We didn't talk much after that. After we finished our snacks, we retrieved our bags and headed into the parlor to do our homework. My mom seemed a little surprised when she walked in and found us silently doing our work, but she didn't say more than 'hello' to each of us before heading to her office.

Nathan stayed for a couple of hours more before he said goodbye to my mom and I walked him back to his house. My mom offered to drive him home, but he declined. Yet, I wasn't about to let him walk home alone, and I could teleport back to my house.

We walked the whole way in silence, not bothering to break it. I think he knew I needed that. More than I needed him to *act* like my friend, I needed him to *be* the friend he had always been to me. Long before we reached his house, the atmosphere between us was more than comforting, as it was full of contentment. It was soothing.

"There you are," Anne sighed when we walked in the front door. "I wondered where you'd gone when Tyler came home without you."

Nathan's voice was wary as he asked, "Where is he?" He tried to hide the surreptitious glance into the living room.

"He went to Rachel's."

It was strange to watch him visibly relax at that knowledge. Just as I was about to ask him what was going on, I remembered that Tyler was the one who threw the drink at me in the movie theater. My first date had happened so long ago that it seemed insignificant now. Of course, it wasn't insignificant to Nathan that his brother was a known adversary of mine.

I couldn't help myself as I scoffed, "You seriously think I have to worry about your brother?"

Nathan shot me an incredulous look. "No, *I* worry about my brother. *You* have a temper. After the movie theater, I think you scare him more than Morgan ever did."

There was no stopping my smug smile after that. "Point well taken."

Anne rolled her eyes. "Are you kids hungry? Alex, did you want to stay for dinner?"

I was about to decline when Nathan gave me an expectant look. "It's only fair. You fed me," he said with a shrug. So I changed my answer.

"I'll have to call my mom and ask."

Anne looked at her son with a pointed expression. "Yes, because that's what you're supposed to do when you're not where your mother expects you to be at certain times," she remarked in a dry tone.

I left them to hash it out while I walked into the living room and picked up the house phone off an end table. My mom was okay with me having dinner with them, so long as I came home right afterward.

At the time, I didn't realize I was setting myself up for a new routine. It didn't bother me when Matt sat with me again in the morning, even though it only lasted a few minutes. I wasn't even that irritated when I found Nathan waiting for me again. That much I had suspected might happen. What I didn't expect was that Matt would miss his stop, and instead kept sitting beside me for the rest of the ride.

I didn't bother to say anything in response when he got off the bus with me. Apparently when Nathan said they'd work something out, it meant more than a seating schedule. Since I knew it wasn't all Matt's fault, just as it wasn't all Nathan's, I figured I'd get them both together at some point and hash out the full details. And throw in a few conditions of my own, if this was to be a regular ordeal.

Of course, by time the following Friday rolled around, I was certain how regular it would be. Which was why I invited them both to get off the bus with me. Something neither of them seemed to have taken into account as a possibility. Either because they'd worked it out to where they never had to have contact with one another, or because they didn't expect me to have a say in the arrangement. No matter what, asking was more of a courtesy than a need. If I was being babysat without my permission, they were coming over whether they liked it or not.

As was habit over the past week and a half, I made them both call their moms while I made our snack. Then I surprised them by heading for the back door as soon as we were done eating. They were so used to homework, they seemed to have forgotten it was the weekend. I hadn't, and the day was nice enough to spend out on the swing.

I'd already kicked off the ground by the time the boys met me under the oak tree. Nathan stood with his arms crossed as he watched me while Matt moved behind me in order to push. By the atmosphere, I could tell they both knew they were in trouble.

"So how long did you plan on keeping this up?" I asked Nathan.

He didn't play dumb like Matt would have. "About a month, to start."

"And after a month?"

Nathan shrugged. "I said 'to start.'"

Grinning a little, I shook my head. "Unapologetic and stubborn. Wonder where you got that from."

His lips twitched a little. "Actually, I learned it from you."

My eyes narrowed and I made a face at him. Behind me, I heard Matt snort a little. As he pushed me once more, I leapt from the swing. Nathan jumped a little and Matt gasped behind me. Not because I jumped, but because I didn't land.

Laughing, I allowed the magick to turn me so I could see both of them at the same time. "What? Oh, stop looking at me like that, Nathan. You remind me of my mom," I grumbled when I saw his unamused expression. "What's the point of having friends that know I can do this, if I can't do it around you guys?"

"A little warning would have been nice."

"Hey, I think it's cool," Matt said, taking my place on the swing. "If I was able to do even a fraction of what you could do, I'd do nothing but use magick all day."

My lips pursed as I studied him. "Do you mind?" I asked before I let the magick seep into him a bit. It searched his person, his blood, his entire being, looking for something it could have latched onto. There was nothing that I could sense that would make it seem as if Matt were capable of manipulating magick.

"That feels weird," he muttered as a shiver ran up his spine.

"Probably because it's not natural for you. Nothing seems to want to attach, so I don't think you could do a fraction of what I could do. Sorry."

"Can you do that to him?" Matt asked, jerking his chin toward Nathan.

My blue eyes met green and we studied each other for a long second, both of us fully aware that Matt didn't know about Nathan's maternal lineage. Without looking away from him, I answered Matt, "Nathan could learn magick if he wanted to."

"But I don't want to," he finished for me.

"Why not?" Matt asked.

Nathan's eyes still didn't leave mine. "Sometimes, being normal is enough. There's nothing that magick could offer me that I couldn't find a way to do without."

I nodded. "Fair enough."

Chapter Twenty Six

SURREAL

My new addition to the weekday rituals soon fell into the boys' routine as well. So much so that all of our parents were well aware what would be happening every week. Of course, I also got payback on them in other ways. Twice in the week, I would get off at one of their houses and do my homework there before heading home for dinner. Nathan's was easier, because I could teleport home from his house-so long as his father and brother didn't see me. When it came to Matt's, however, I had to walk to the end of the block before blinking between places.

Fridays and Saturdays belonged at my house, though. Most of the Fridays we'd just hang out until they had to go home, but on Saturday I took them through the woods to the lake. Each time we reached the point where my original path to Morgan's branched off of the lake path, my chest tightened a little and I was forced to look away. More than once, when this happened, one of the boys would throw an arm over my shoulders and steer me away.

It wasn't until the one week that Matt wasn't with us that I took Nathan into the woods and stopped where the paths split. The police were done with Morgan's cottage, I knew. I could go back whenever I wanted. Neither Anne nor Sarah would stop me. And I had Nathan.

My teeth dug into my bottom lip as I wondered whether or not I was ready to do this. I hadn't been to the cottage since my Ascension over two months ago. Same with the circle. One way or the other, I would soon have to go to both places, as the Samhain celebration was only a few days away. Besides, the cats could have been feral for all I knew, at this point.

"Don't do that, Lex," Nathan murmured.

Startled, my eyes shot up to his. "Do what?"

His eyes were full of compassion as he answered, "Talk yourself into going. If you want to go, we'll go. But if you don't want to, there's no reason for you to have to."

My brows furrowed as I tried to remember if I'd been speaking aloud. I knew I hadn't been. Which meant either my face was that easy to read, or there was something Nathan was picking up on that was more mental than physical. Thinking back to my Wiccaning, I knew my telepathy flared to life then. Would the same happen if Nathan had been blessed at the circle?

"No, Nathan, I do have to go. But the 'when' is up to me. I think now may be it. While I still have the nerve to do it."

"Okay. Do you want me to come with you?"

I smiled, glad for his compassion. I knew if I said 'no' he would stand in that very spot until I came back for him. Lucky for us both, I answered, "Yes. I'm pretty sure I'm going to need you there with me."

Nathan returned my smile and said, "Okay." Then we started down the other path.

It was surreal, returning to the cottage. Everything seemed still and silent. As if it were all in a state of stasis. Where everything was sleeping until kissed by magick once more.

"It feels like it's waiting for something," I murmured to Nathan as we traversed the back garden. The energy the plants usually gave off was harbored inside of them now, gathering in their roots and spreading through the soil, leaving the air feeling a bit stale.

"It's waiting for you."

There was something in his voice that made me turn. "What do you mean?"

Without missing a beat, Nathan asked, "Did you ever doubt it? You belong to this place as much as it belongs to you, Lex. Who else would it be waiting for?"

Before I could answer, something triggered in my senses and my eyes shot toward where the oleander plant used to be. A big, gaping hole existed there now and the flow of energy in the garden soil was disrupted by its absence. It felt like a fist squeezed my heart as I realized they took the whole plant as evidence.

Shaking my head, I could feel the anger building inside of me. Louder than the questions, stronger than the fear, and full of the pain of the past few weeks. It was bad enough that my best friend had taken her own life, but to be accused of ending it was the last straw.

My body vibrated until I could no longer stand. Dropping to my knees in the soil, I cradled my head in my hands and curled my body over my thighs. I was doing my best to contain the rage, afraid of what would happen if I released it. What damage could I do?

Beside me, Nathan kneeled down and placed a hand on my back. When I didn't shrug him away, he began rubbing up and down on either side of my spine. Unbeknownst to him, he was pouring a little of his own magick into me. Soothing, calming, contented magick. Much like his mother, Nathan had a gift for making people feel better.

Just not Morgan.

The scream was ripped from my body. Torn from the depths of my being as I was hunched in on myself. Fury erupted from my throat, tearing the vocal chords as it went. Even as I kept a stopper on my destructive, vengeful magick, my body gave way to the only release I didn't bother to control. So I screamed. Again and again and again. Until my throat was raw and the soil under my knees was wet with my tears.

With the rage expelled, only the grief was left to tug at my shoulders and twist my stomach. To create a hollowness in my chest that was speared through whenever I took a breath. The tears wouldn't stop flowing, though I couldn't imagine I had much water left in my system.

Throughout it all, Nathan just sat next to me and rubbed my back. Didn't say a word, not even to try and soothe me. He just let me scream and cry while maintaining our customary silence. It was in that moment that I realized how much I had to be grateful for. People as caring as Nathan didn't show up every day, and I was blessed to have him as my friend.

My best friend.

In that moment, Nathan became more than my last vestige of Morgan. He also became a last vestige of me. I could trust him with part of myself-the part he already took for himself-and know that it couldn't be any safer. Nathan would guard that part of me with his life.

And when this was all over, I knew he would help me remember who I was before. He would teach me how to be me again, once I got over how broken Morgan left me. That was the reason Nathan was in my life, and I couldn't be more grateful.

That was the first night Nathan slept over at my house. He let me lean on him the whole way back to my house and my mom took one look at us and agreed to his request. A decision my dad was vehemently against as he and my mom argued in hissing whispers while she prepared one of the guest bedrooms. She won in the end, however, and I knew my dad didn't sleep at all that night. It was almost amusing to think that, if it weren't a safety violation, he would have locked me in my room. Especially since he seemed to have forgotten that I could use magick.

Nathan made up for some of it, however, by helping my mom with breakfast. Though I'm not sure Nathan realized it, he also earned a grudging amount of my dad's respect by not sneaking out of his room at all in the middle of the night. That still wasn't an open invitation to spend the weekends with us.

As I was getting ready to walk him home, my dad's eyes narrowed in a way that suggested he wouldn't survive it if my dad saw him in his house for the rest of the day. I smiled to let him know that I got the message before I ushered Nathan out. It vanished as soon as the heavy door closed behind us.

We began our walk with our silence, but it wasn't the amicable, contented kind that usually hovered around us. Instead, my nerves spread it taut and I could feel Nathan's expectation coating the strands like dew on a spiderweb. At last, I took a deep breath and said, "I'm sorry for yesterday."

The tension snapped like a rubber band as we both relaxed a bit. "Don't be, Lex. You needed a moment and you took it. That's what you're supposed to do."

My heart felt lighter for a moment, but crashed back into my chest with a heavy thump. Then I admitted, "I put you in danger by having you there, Nathan. I got so angry and hurt and I could barely keep a hold on my magick. If I hadn't…"

"You could have caused some damage. I understand, Lex. Really, I do. But you didn't lose control and you didn't hurt anyone or anything. You're fine, and so am I. It's over, with no harm done."

I tried to smile at him. "Thanks. Could we not tell Matt? I know he knows a lot, but there are some things even he wouldn't understand."

His lips pulled up into a half-smile. "No problem."

I smiled back, but looked straight ahead as I added, "I'm also sorry for my dad sitting outside your bedroom door all night."

Nathan laughed a little. "It wasn't all night. Was it?"

We laughed together and continued on. Our normal silence fell over us in gentle layers. Hidden within it was the vow we had built our friendship upon: that we would have each other's backs, no matter what.

Chapter Twenty Seven

RESTLESS

In the two months following my return to Morgan's cottage, I had righted the cottage and the garden as much as I was able. It took more magick than I thought it would to undo all of the damage the police and forensics teams had inflicted, but it also seemed to help whenever I had Nathan with me. On Samhain and Yule, I discharged my duties at the circle, whose neutrality did not give it the same air of stasis as the cottage. It did not care whether or not I was there or working magick with it; in itself it was a place of power, but without care as to how that power was used.

Within that same timeframe, Nathan had slept over at my house two more times, which my dad was very grudging about. Matt also slept over once, but my father wasn't a fan of his due to the fact that we had dated. Then, one night about a week before Yule, my parents granted me one sleepover while they treated themselves to a date night.

"You realize my only friends are male, right?" I asked my mom when she brought it up.

She rolled her eyes. "We trust you, and the boys, not to do anything stupid."

"You just don't want me left alone in the house overnight. You know I can take care of myself, Mom. I'm not weak."

"Being cautious is never a weakness, Alexandria. And this has nothing to do with us doubting your capabilities or trying to treat you like a child. This is a boon. From father to daughter. It's one night for the three of you to have the run of the house without turning your father's hair prematurely gray. Now say 'thank you' and call the boys."

I smiled a little for her benefit, expressed my gratitude in a hug, and went for the phone. So it was that, come that Saturday, Anne dropped off both Nathan and Matt in the late afternoon. I think it bothered Nathan more than he let on when I sent him and Matt inside while I talked to his mom for a bit.

"Any idea what's going to happen with the police? I get interviewed almost weekly. Still," I sighed.

Anne shook her head. "They used to stop by to question me, but once they learned how firmly I believed Morgan's death was a suicide, their visits became far less. You know, I see on the news all the time how people are so eager for answers and have to push law enforcement to keep a case open. Now, with an obvious case of suicide before them, our police cannot seem to let it go."

A shiver traveled up my spine. "It's me they want. They can't handle what I am."

"You're different, Alex. That's all. But you are right in saying that they do want you. Whether it's because of the Craft or the fact that it is screwing up their facts, I'm not sure. Without substantial proof that she committed suicide, however, you will be a person of interest in this case for a long time. Why couldn't she just leave a note like a normal person?"

A smile pulled at my lips. "For that reason

alone: she was not normal. Thank you, Anne. I'll see you tomorrow."

"Goodnight, Alex. Keep my kid out of trouble," she teased, knowing exactly who played the role of bodyguard.

I said goodbye and went back into the house and found Matt and Nathan in the doorway to the family room. As soon as I walked in, Matt raised his eyebrows at me. "Do we get to stay up late, *Mom*?"

Rolling my eyes, I remarked, "Only if you behave. Did you guys see the pizza in the kitchen or not?"

"Pizza?" Matt spun in place and marched off down the hall. Nathan and I grinned and followed.

My parents waved goodbye while the three of us gorged ourselves in the kitchen. Once they were gone, we grabbed bags of popcorn, chips, and a couple of other snacks I'd gotten in preparation and took them all into the family room. Then we took turns picking movies out of the stack Nathan had rented.

By the time we were halfway through the third movie, it was well past sunset and we called a halt for bathroom breaks. While Matt headed upstairs and Nathan proceeded toward the kitchen, I found myself drifting toward the parlor. Movies were all well and good when one was in the mood to watch them, but the one we were on was rather boring, so I was growing restless.

In response to some of my mood, a fire flared to life in the parlor's fireplace and I drifted toward the comforting crackle and pop of the flames eating at the wood. My eyes stared into the flames, watching as images danced into view before flickering away once more. As I stood there, a haunting melody started roving through my head. Before I could stop myself, I found myself at the piano, my fingers traveling over the keys in a lullaby that would haunt me for the rest of my life.

Nathan abandoned whatever he was doing in the kitchen the moment the first note drifted through the house. I could feel him approaching in his usual, determined stride. Matt, on the other hand, crept from the bathroom upstairs and was wary about making his way down the stairs. They both stopped in the doorway and allowed me to finish the melody.

As the last note lingered, Nathan cleared his throat and asked, "Where did you learn that, Lex?"

I turned my head to meet his knowing gaze. "Alyssa Rice. She learned it from Victoria. Morgan's birth mother."

The shiver that ran up his spine was so subtle, I would never have detected the motion before my Ascension. As it was, I knew why he had asked and so his reaction was predictable. The lullaby had belonged to Morgan's family. Which meant that it belonged to him, too.

Matt, unaware of much of the significance of what I'd just said, shook his head and sighed. "The dead girl," he muttered. "How'd I know. Does anything normal happen around you?"

At that, I grinned. "What fun would that be?"

In an instant, the fire died, casting the room in a blanket of shadows while I disappeared. Appearing in the family room, I giggled a little to tease the boys. As soon as they turned to look, I jumped into the kitchen, rustling the bags of chips to let them know where I was.

"Very funny," Matt called.

"Is to me," I said, popping in on the stairs behind them. Before I could teleport anywhere else, however, Nathan twisted in place and grabbed my wrist. "Hey," I yelped as he dragged me toward him.

Then Matt dug his fingers into my sides and I jerked. I fell back on the stairs with Nathan still holding my wrist and Matt still tickling me. After a few seconds, I ripped my wrist out of Nathan's grip and kicked out at Matt, causing him to jump back out of striking distance. Panting with laughter, I hauled myself halfway up the stairs where they couldn't reach me. All three of us collapsed where we were, laughing so hard our sides were hurting.

"You earned that," Nathan managed a few minutes later.

"Yeah, yeah," I muttered, sticking my tongue out at him.

"What was that even about?" Matt asked.

I shrugged. "Not sure. I feel odd tonight. Restless."

"Somehow I feel like changing the movie isn't going to help anything," Matt grumbled.

Nathan waited a heartbeat later before suggesting, "Let's go to the lake."

"What?" Matt and I asked in unison.

He shrugged. "Why not? You can bring us back long before your parents get home. It'll do you some good to get fresh air."

The smile curled up my lips while Matt's eyebrows rose. Before I could even answer, he sighed, "Let me get my coat."

A few minutes later, the three of us were standing in front of the lake. A frigid wind rolled in over the frozen water the moment we got there, causing Matt to shoot a glare my way. I didn't care, though. Nathan was right, this was where I needed to be.

Taking a deep breath, I walked down past the log where Matt and I used to sit and kicked off my boots. With the cold seeping up through the soles of my feet, I raised my head and found the visions of Victoria and Freyja walking past me into the water. Around my neck, the watch's ticking grew louder and the metal felt warm against my skin.

The ice at the edge of the lake was thin and broken close to the shore. There was just enough space for me to stand with my toes in the water. My mouth fell open in a gasp as new images blasted through me.

The onslaught came to a close with a vision of the woman who'd ordered Mary Sullivan's burning, Margarite. She stood smiling at me as if we were the best of friends, while two young girls splashed in the crystalline water. My throat constricted as my gaze landed on the toddler kicking at water that was up to her rounded belly. She looked so happy, I couldn't help but smile.

It struck me in an instant that the little girl was Mary Sullivan's daughter. A bond was forged the moment I looked at her, and I knew what it was to be a mother in that instant. The love I felt for that baby girl compared to nothing else I'd ever experienced.

Tears escaped my eyes, creating silent trails down my face, as I continued to watch her. It was a vision that refused to dissipate until I felt Nathan step close to me. Another wave of emotion shot through me and I gasped as I turned toward him. For that one fraction of a second, it wasn't Nathan's face I saw. Then blue eyes darkened to emerald green and I was no longer entrapped by the magick of the lake.

"Lex," he whispered as his hand brushed against mine, "it's been an hour. We have to get back."

Drawing in a deep breath, I felt the cold for the first time since we arrived. Backing out of the water, I was shivering hard. Between Matt and Nathan, I found myself seated on the log while they put my boots back on my feet.

It took a few minutes for me to get my bearings. When I did, I realized how right Nathan was. Midnight was nearing and my parents would be home soon. As soon as I felt up to it, I reached my hands out to Nathan and Matt. The minute they took them, we blinked from the lake to the foyer.

Nathan helped me out of my coat and my boots. If I wasn't so cold, I'd have scolded him for treating me like a little kid. At the same time, Matt ran upstairs and grabbed a blanket out of the linen closet and flew back down the stairs. I rolled my eyes as they ushered me back into the family room where I lit the fire in the fireplace and the three of us gathered around in front of it. After a while, our eyes drifted shut and we fell asleep leaning on each other.

I jerked a little when I heard the front door open and close. The hallway light flicked on and I heard my parents talking to one another as they entered the house. After an immediate evaluation of my circumstances–my head resting on Nathan's shoulder as we leaned back against the couch where Matt was stretched out, snoring–I decided it was in my best interest to feign sleep.

"That girl," my mother chuckled. "A movie has nothing on a fire to that child."

"Oh no," my dad groaned as he spotted our sleeping forms.

"Don't. Leave them be. There's no point sending them up to bed now."

"And Lex?"

I could imagine my mom rolling her eyes. "Leave her. It's not going to do her any harm to have one night with them. Not when we both know how little she'll see of them once this year is over."

My dad sighed but must have nodded his agreement since they flicked off the light and headed upstairs. As soon as they were gone, my head jerked up and I stared after them.

What did that mean? That I wouldn't get to see the boys once the year was over?

My heart sank as realization set in. Of course. My dad had almost moved us because of the Alyssa Rice incident. After my mentor's suicide and murder investigation, we were getting out of this town as soon as this whole ordeal was cleared up.

Tears burned behind my eyelids as I turned away. My eyes found Nathan's in the gloom and I put a hand over my mouth to stifle the sob. He didn't say anything. Just wrapped an arm around my shoulders and pulled me to him. Pulling the blanket up to hide my face, I sobbed against him.

Everything was falling apart.

Chapter Twenty Eight

CHARGED

I didn't realize how right I was until almost five months later. After so long, I thought that they were finally reaching the end of the investigation. They had nothing on me, when it came down to it. There was no way to prove that what I said wasn't true. By the beginning of May, I had grown complacent.

That was a mistake.

Nathan and I were sitting in our homeroom when a girl with a note walked in. If she wasn't blasting nervous energy my way, I might not have known that I was the reason she was there. As it was, I cut off my conversation with Nathan and snapped my eyes up to lock on hers. She stumbled as she walked and the teacher almost had to catch her before she could hand over the note. When she turned away, she was shaking like a leaf.

"Alexandria Ryder, you are wanted in the office."

I barely heard my teacher's reedy voice as my vision shot across the school and found the two detectives waiting for me. Instead of feeling upset or derisive, I found myself filled with relief. They had made their move. At last.

"No," I stated before the girl could make good on her escape. As if she knew I was speaking to her, she stopped at the door and turned to face me. "If they want me, they can come and get me."

Wide-eyed, the girl gave a hurried bob of her head before darting out of the room. When I was sure she was heading back to the office, my gaze refocused to find everyone in my class staring at me. Nathan's gaze was the hardest to ignore as it pressed in on me in a knowing manner. For a moment, I let myself be distracted by the emerald facets of his irises and kept myself from hearing the thoughts he was throwing at me.

We were still staring at one another when Detectives Ross and Stone entered the classroom. Their eyes locked on mine after a moment's perusal and Detective Ross barked my name as they began their approach. I rose up out of my chair. Nathan moved faster, springing to his feet and turning to put himself between me and the detectives.

Before he could cause a scene, I grabbed hold of his arm and pulled until he glanced down at me. My eyes pleaded with him even as I murmured, "Call your Aunt Sarah. Tell her what's happening. Then call my mom."

Both detectives scowled as they reached us, their eyes unleashing veiled threats as they looked at Nathan. My best friend raised his chin and stared defiantly back at them. Then he stepped aside, so he could watch and report everything he saw in the moments to come.

"Alexandria Ryder, could you please come with us?" Detective Stone asked, holding up his hand toward the door.

This time, I raised my chin. "You know better than that, Detective. If I'm not under arrest, I'm not going anywhere with you. Do it here and now, or don't make this mistake at all."

Detective Ross scowled and stepped toward me. "Alexandria Ryder, you are under arrest for the murder of Morgan LeFayette. Turn around and place your hands behind your back."

I did as he asked and felt a sickening dread in my stomach as the handcuffs snapped into place. My teeth ground together with every crank of the metallic teeth, but I didn't try to test my restraints. They couldn't hold me if I didn't want them to, but I didn't need the detectives to know that.

Then Detective Stone announced, "You have the right to remain silent. If you give up that right, anything you say can and will be used against you in a court of law. You have the right to have an attorney present during questioning. If you cannot afford an attorney, one will be provided for you by the courts. Do you understand these rights as I have read them to you?"

"Yes."

The detectives steered me toward the door of the classroom and I felt Nathan following on our heels. While we made our way to the exit, Nathan darted into the office.

That was when it hit me: this was really happening. I was being charged with my best friend's murder.

Detective Ross escorted me to a cinder block room with a camera in an upper corner. It was a cramped space with very little room. Not at all like what people saw on TV. I almost wished it had the dual-sided glass mirror, because then it would almost seem like a joke. I wasn't that lucky.

While Detective Stone was busy with something else, Detective Ross uncuffed me and had me take a seat. For a while, we sat in silence. He didn't try to ask me any questions, and I didn't volunteer anything of my own. Leaning back in his chair, he tried to pass himself off as nonchalant and uncaring as to the outcome. I, on the other hand, reacted as any surly teenager would and leaned back in my chair with my arms crossed in front of my chest.

A few minutes later, Detective Stone entered the room, carrying a couple of cups of coffee and a can of soda which he set on the table in front of me. I didn't even shift as my eyes followed him to the second chair. For a second, he looked between his partner and myself, getting his bearings.

"So, Alex, you understand why you're here, don't you? You understand why we had to bring you in."

He wasn't asking and I was fighting hard not to curl my lip in disgust. It burned, in an acidic, volatile way, that they couldn't see Morgan's death as the suicide it was. Even working with only the facts to guide them–as they were obviously doing–should have led them to that conclusion. Yet, I couldn't help but feel as though I was targeted. That, no matter the reality behind the case, I still would have found myself in this position.

The hair rose on the back of my neck as I pondered that. Something was wrong about the entire situation, and I couldn't help but wonder: why now? What had they found to convince them that they could arrest me? What did they have that would cause someone to issue a warrant for my arrest? It made no sense.

Realizing that I wasn't about to respond to his statements, Detective Stone opened his mouth again, only for a knock on the door to cause his teeth to snap shut. He sent one inquisitive look at his partner before Detective Ross opened the door. On the other side of the officer who'd knocked stood Sarah. A smile tugged at my lips, which prompted Detective Stone to turn around.

"Mrs. Thompson," Detective Ross said. If he were wearing a hat, I swear he would have tipped it to her as she stepped forward.

"I'm sorry, Mrs. Thompson," Detective Stone stated, stepping forward so that the two men created a wall between her and me, "but there is an interrogation in process. We've taken a suspect into custody concerning your mother's murder."

"That's hard to do when there was never a murder committed, don't you think, gentlemen? Now I'll ask you to step out of the room while I console my client for this wrongful imprisonment." I couldn't stop the grin forming as her casual tone drifted past them. Both men looked dumbfounded.

"You are representing Alexandria Ryder?" Detective Ross demanded, his face becoming a thunderhead in an instant.

"I am."

"She's being charged with your mother's murder," he hissed, losing all composure in an instant.

I caught a glimpse of Sarah's hair as she flipped it over one shoulder. "Alleged murder. Now are you going to allow me access to my client, or are you willing to violate all the rights of a teenager? I would decide quickly, if I were you. Mrs. Ryder is on her way."

"Fifteen minutes should suffice," Detective Stone said in a forced calm voice.

Detective Ross stalked out so that I was able to see Sarah's smirk as she answered, "I'll inform you when we're ready for your interview." The detective's shoulders straightened as he strode out of the room. Sarah locked the door even as her eyes shot to the camera. A second later, the red 'recording' light went out.

"We won't have much time, they'll turn it back on in fifteen minutes just to spite me, even though they wouldn't be able to use a second of it in court. Now tell me what happened," she urged as she took a seat. In a few minutes, I was able to explain everything, and after a few questions and a minor scolding, I told her about the interviews they'd performed at my house.

"That's all? Everything?"

"That's all. Sarah, I don't understand what's going on. Why now? What do they think they've found that would lead them to arrest me?"

Sarah drew herself upright and I knew right then that whatever she said was going to set me off. Putting a hasty cap on my magick, I growled, "Tell me what you know."

Nodding once, she announced, "My mother left you everything in her will. All of her possessions, the cottage, the property. Everything. Part of her money was separated into trusts for her grandchildren, but the rest was left to you."

My mouth fell open and my eyes grew wide. It felt as if someone had punched me in the stomach and all of the air whooshed out of my lungs. At the same time, a dull headache formed behind my ears and I could hear Nathan's voice from when I went back to the cottage before Mabon.

'You belong to this place as much as it belongs to you.'

I shook my head, a few curse words flying through my mind. "Nathan knew, didn't he?" She nodded. "And you told him not to tell me," I accused. Sarah didn't bother to deny it. Rolling my eyes, I asked, "So that's why they decided to arrest me? Because they think I have a motive?"

Sarah's expression became a little more guarded. "Not exactly." Taking a deep breath, she went on, "They recently acquired Morgan's journal."

Chapter Twenty Nine

DUE TIME

My eyes narrowed and my temperature spiked. "They have her Book of Shadows?"

"No. Her journal. The one she sent to me and I mailed to the detectives."

"You did *what*?"

"Hear me out," she urged as I was building up steam for the explosion that was about to occur. Against my better judgment, my jaw snapped shut and I glared at her. "I knew it could go either way. They would read it and decide to dismiss the charges, or they would indict you."

"Why would you do that?" I hissed.

"Because I want this to go to trial."

The air whooshed out of my lungs once more. She wanted this to happen? For my life to get smeared and torn apart? For the truth about her own mother to come out, when she had to use her sister's spell to make people forget that she was the witch's daughter? What was she thinking?

"Why? Why would you do this to me?" I whispered, horrified.

"Not *to* you, Alex. *For* you. So you don't have to run from this the way Anne and I have."

"No. You would rather have the whole town believe me to be a murderer," I scoffed.

"No. I would rather the town learn what it means to be a witch and to live by a creed. You will be acquitted, Alexandria. That I can guarantee."

"How?"

"Because my mother committed suicide. And I know why."

In an instant, my indignation vanished. The hole gaping in my chest thrummed in response, eager for an answer. An explanation. Something. Anything that would explain why she left me.

I begged her for that answer. With my expression and my mind, I said what I couldn't force out of my throat. For several long minutes, I pleaded with Sarah to reveal to me what she knew. Yet, she wouldn't budge.

All in due time, she answered.

I deserve to know.

And you will learn. When it is time.

"Why are you doing this to me?" I whispered again.

"Maybe it's not about you," she whispered back. "Maybe it's about the people of Cedar Creek. Maybe it's about prejudice and false assumptions. Maybe it's about them learning how to treat those who are different. And maybe for them to learn that, it has to be you to teach them."

"And maybe I don't care, Sarah."

"You do. You were trained by my mother. You don't have a choice."

She was right. I did care. Not because the opinions of those living in Cedar Creek mattered to me, but because they deserved to know how wrong they were. They deserved to face the consequences of their actions. And maybe it took a witch trial for them to learn that how they had treated me and Morgan was not okay.

Taking a deep breath, I raised my eyes to Sarah's and nodded. "What do you want me to do?"

The detectives questioned me for hours. At first, it covered the same ground we'd been over months in advance. Then it started to shift toward reasons why I might have wanted Morgan dead. They were both surprised when they asked when I learned of the will and I told them that Sarah had just informed me of it. When they were satisfied that I wasn't lying about it, they then began questioning me about Morgan's journal. It took them much longer to believe I had no clue what they were talking about.

At the end of the interview, I was allowed to see my parents for a few brief moments–with the camera turned on–before they took me away to be booked. My arraignment wasn't for another hour, but Sarah had said she would try to get me sent home with them, though we both had little hope for it. Then I was sent on my way with a growing sense of horror spreading throughout my system.

It felt so wrong to be fingerprinted. I dipped my fingers as lightly into the ink as I could, but it sunk in when each finger was pressed into the card. When the officer released my hand, I found black smudges smeared all over the place.

Afterward, I was shoved in front of a camera and had a mug shot taken. I felt humiliated and enraged. Around me, the lights started flickering and a grim smile pulled at my lips when people turned to stare at me. Then I was given a jumpsuit to change into and taken to a cell in order to wait for my arraignment.

For several long minutes, I could do nothing but pace. The energy building inside of me flared in several magickal outbursts that I refused to control. If they didn't want to believe what I was capable of, that was their problem. And if they wanted a demonstration, I was more than ready to give it to them, no matter what Sarah advised.

After a while, I whirled around and went to sit on the bench against the wall. Holding my hands in front of me, I focused on the ink staining my skin. I took a breath and began to draw the ink out of the skin, watching as a ball of black liquid began to coalesce in front of my eyes. When the last vestiges of it were released from my hands, I hurled the ball through the bars and watched with pleasure as it splattered against the cinder block wall.

Shortly after that, a guard walked in and saw what I'd done. As he had no idea how I did it, however, he chose to say nothing about it and instead took me to my arraignment. It didn't take long and it ended how Sarah and I thought it would anyway. When the charge is first degree murder, they don't see how it's safe for the public to send that person home.

After that, things moved rather slowly for me. To the prosecution, however, it must have seemed fast. Sarah insisted on a speedy trial, so the preliminary hearings and such all came about within the next few weeks. At first, the judge questioned her haste, seeing as he believed she didn't have enough time to prepare a proper defense for me. However, she had been investigating her mother's suicide for as long as the cops had been trying to find evidence to indict me for murder. She was more than prepared; she was ready and willing.

All the while, I languished in a juvenile detention center. It was different, being with other kids who had done some legitimately awful things to people. All the same, they learned not to bother with me. A few glamours of people they'd hurt served to make that an easy affair.

It also helped that I could astral project, or I might have actually killed someone while I was locked up. As it was, I got out every night. The first time I did it, I about gave my mother a heart attack, until I explained all about astral projections and how I was still there as well as with her. It'd taken all night to convince my parents that no one would know, before they relented. The next time, I drifted out at lunch time in order to prove to them that no one noticed that I wasn't all there.

During quite a few mealtimes, I dropped in on Anne. She was a stay-at-home mom, so she was glad that I visited her during the day. I was even learning to cook in the times I allotted for spending with her. It was strange, how much of a shift our relationship took. After a while, I couldn't help but think of her as a second mom.

Matt was harder to pin down times for. While I was almost always able to find him in his room after school, it was not the most tolerable timeframe. Especially after I appeared once while he was getting dressed after a shower. That was more awkward than either of us would have admitted to, but we laughed it off soon enough.

Nathan had the opposite story. Any time after school was ideal, but the where presented a challenge. Sometimes I found him in his bedroom–usually later in the evening. Other times, I was surprised when he showed up at my house. Once, he was even mowing the lawn–being careful to miss the flower beds and herb patches, I noticed. Then there were the times I found him at Morgan's.

"The trial starts tomorrow," I announced as I appeared in the main room. "And I think this counts as trespassing."

Nathan looked over his shoulder at me and rolled his eyes before going back to scooping cat food out into a bowl. "I call it house-sitting. And cat-sitting. Actually, I really should be getting paid for this," he said as he set the bowl on the floor beneath the table. As one, the small horde of cats descended on it. They would crunch and chomp for about an hour before he turned them out of the house-litter boxes were the one thing neither us nor the cats would abide by.

"The check's in the mail," I answered with

a grin as he took a seat on the bench. Morgan's chair was left to itself as I reclined in Alyssa's rocking chair.

He shot me a half-smile before asking, "So where are you right now?"

Part of me shot back over the distance. "Being transferred back to the jail. The center is too far away to accommodate transporting me for the trial."

"You've got time then."

I smiled a little. "It's a two-hour drive," I reminded him. Of course, that was the reason that no one had come to visit; other than my own capabilities making it a moot point.

"Want to go to the lake?"

The lake. Of course. Because if he wasn't home, at my house, or at the cottage, he was at the lake. My head tilted to the side and I began a thorough study of him. There was magick inside of him, no doubt, but it wasn't magick that was kin to water. Victoria and even Freyja had had an affinity with the liquid element, but Nathan didn't seem to. Instead, deep within him was a soft, steady thrum as if from a heartbeat. It wasn't emotional or turbulent like water, fiery and passionate like fire, or drifted with air's distracted dance. Earth elements were always the most steady of those who worked magick and it somehow didn't surprise me at all to find that Nathan belonged to that brand. Yet...

"The lake calls to you, doesn't it?"

He shrugged. "Strange, right? When two of my relatives drowned there. Seems the two things my family have in common is suicidal tendencies and that lake."

I didn't like the way he said that and my frown must have tipped him off. Holding up his hands in a halting gesture, he backtracked, "Not me, Lex. Promise. Just thinking about Morgan and the other two."

"Victoria and Freyja," I reminded him in a low tone.

He nodded. "Yeah."

We didn't say anything else for a while. Neither of us wanted to expand on a conversation that was not only morbid but struck too close to my own circumstances. After a bit, I stood up and nodded my head toward the door. Leaving it cracked so that the cats could filter out as they wished, we headed down to the lake.

Not much else was said between us as we sat side by side and stared out over the water. Then he asked me why the water wasn't poisoned by Victoria and Freyja's bodies. To which I answered, "Magick." And just when I was getting ready to leave, he said, "By the way, the lake is yours now, too. Morgan owned it before. So, I guess we've all been trespassing for a while."

I didn't have a chance to respond before I faded back into my body. For which he should have been grateful. It was getting to be frustrating having his family spring things on me every time I turned around.

Chapter Thirty

TRIAL

There have been few instances in my life where I have felt so small and insignificant. All of which were Morgan's fault. Including sitting at a polished wooden table in a large, forbidding courtroom. It was one of many times that I damned her for not leaving a suicide note.

The first day of the trial was the hardest. The prosecutor, Angela Garder, looked every bit the logical, put together woman in front of the jury. She spoke in a clear, concise tone, and seemed to believe everything she said. Even if none of it was true.

"Ladies and gentlemen of the jury," Garder began, "you are all asked here today to see that justice is done. Justice for a woman of means who, out of the goodness of her heart, took a stranger into her home and treated her as a member of her family, and paid for it with her life. I ask you all now to take a good look at the Defendant, Alexandria Ryder. She looks like a harmless enough young woman, but with the facts presented to you, you will find as the rest of us have, that thirteen is not too young to commit murder.

"Mind, it is facts of this that you will be presented. The Defense, of course, will attempt to lead you astray with fairy tales of rituals and magic. In this way, they will attempt to dissuade you from the facts of the case and present you with a fantastical version of events, as created by an imaginative young woman. I know that you will see through this charade to the heart of the matter. Which is: Alexandria Ryder did knowingly and willfully poison her mentor, Morgan LeFayette. Now we ask that you give us the justice we are seeking for this woman whose only crime was to care too much for a girl she barely knew."

Then it was Sarah's turn. Rising to her feet, she moved to stand before the jury with her hands behind her back. Her smile was grim as she nodded her head in greeting to the jurors before she spread them wide and sighed, "Ladies and gentlemen of the jury, I apologize for what you are about to endure. It is not every day that a case like this comes before the court, and I am sorry that it is my client's case in particular that you should be wasting your time with. For the simple truth of the matter is: Morgan Le-Fayette took her own life, using a plant in her own garden, and prepared into a tea by her own hand. If my client had been aware of what was about to happen that August evening, she would have tried to stop her. This we will prove, using the very same facts that the Prosecution will present to you, as well as a few that they never even thought to look for. We will not only give you facts to accept, but the truth that goes with them. No matter how unbelievable it may seem."

It was begun.

The Prosecution spent the next three days presenting their case, and I could now see why the detectives had been on me from the beginning. If I were to look at it taking in only the evidence and their testimony, I might have doubted events as well.

As it was, the first thing they did was bring

out the recording of the emergency call I'd made following Morgan's suicide. Short and deliberate as it had been, there wasn't much for them to go off of. Although, if they'd listened to the one I'd made about Alyssa Rice four years ago, they'd be less apt to judge. Maybe.

After that, they put the responding officers on the stand as well as the EMTs. Each one testified first as to my reaction to having them there and all of what they could remember me saying. The EMTs testified as to what they had determined to be time of death and how they had felt the scene had been staged and that a team needed to be called in right away to investigate the site as a potential murder.

With the cops on the stand, Sarah didn't get much out of them except that they agreed that I seemed to be in shock. She even got them to admit to what they saw after Anne and Nathan arrived and how I'd reacted in my grief-stricken state. It took everything I had not to turn around and look at where Nathan had snuck into the back of the courtroom.

From the two EMTs she got their pointed admission that they could not disprove that suicide was the cause of death. Nor were they trained to come to such decisions when responding to a call of this nature. One even slipped up and talked about prolonged states of shock being possible and highly probable if someone witnessed a suicide. Which almost made Garder's face turn red, I was sure.

When they were finished, Garder put both detectives on the stand and played a few recordings of my interviews with them. I restrained myself as I tried to smile, glad that I had thought to record the same interviews and had given the footage to Sarah. While Ross and Stone were testifying, Garder divulged the bulk of the evidence held against me. The motive was a minor thing to them, as they believed the facts were all that were needed to find me guilty. Yet, the amount left to me in the will, as opposed to her blood relatives, seemed to speak for itself. Then they announced the date she had changed the will and my stomach churned.

"March twenty-fourth," Detective Ross stated with some triumph as he looked to me. He knew it was the day after my birthday. What he didn't know was that it was the day after my vision. On my thirteenth birthday, I had informed Morgan that I would Ascend that summer. She'd changed her will the next day so that I would be taken care of when she died. Because she knew exactly when that would happen, too.

Morgan planned this, I mentally hissed at Sarah.

Even her thoughts were unperturbed as she answered, *I know.*

On cross examination, of course, she made sure to ask him when he had informed me of the will. He looked a little sullen when he mentioned that he never had. When she asked him when he had questioned me about it, he seemed more than a little inadequate when he answered with the date of my arrest. With something as large as a lake for a motive, it was a little suspicious why it had never been brought up in the interviews they'd had with me.

"Then what was the point of all those interviews? Weren't you visiting my client on a regular basis to glean information? If you weren't questioning her about the will she had no clue about, then what were you questioning her about?"

"The things she described just weren't possible. Clearly, she was lying. Before we brought up new information, we were hoping she would tell us the truth of the facts we already knew."

"You were hoping she would change her story."

"Yes. We were waiting for the moment she slipped."

"Did she, Detective? Did Miss Ryder ever change her story?"

A sullen expression crept across his face as he admitted, "No, she did not."

Sarah nodded as if to herself. "Tell me Detective, can you perform a cartwheel?"

He snorted. "No."

"Neither can I," Sarah answered. "Do you believe cartwheels are impossible to perform?"

His eyes narrowed. "No."

Again, she nodded. "So, what you're saying is, even though it is impossible for you or I to do, there are those in the world who turn perfectly good cartwheels, correct?" Detective Ross glared at her and she gave him a thin-lipped smile. "No need to answer, Detective."

There were several more witnesses that Sarah went at with subtle barbs and determined statements that always seemed to elicit more information than the witness intended to give. Not to say that the Prosecution wasn't making its case. Discounting everything I was capable of, Garder was making her case with the things that had seemed so insignificant before.

My silence seemed to be the most damning. Because I refused to release the location of where Morgan died, and they had been unable to find it after a thorough search of the woods–to which Sarah asked how they would know if they had found it–I was made to look uncooperative and secretive. Which I was, to be fair, but not because I killed my mentor.

Beyond the will and my silence, the physical evidence was almost nonexistent. The entire case seemed built around how one could interpret evidence to fit their own ideas of what happened. The truth was that Morgan had committed suicide, yet the way her cloak was wrapped, the fact that she was wet, and the three-hour gap between her death and my phone call was pretty damning in itself. Then we got to the journal and I felt myself interested to know not only what was inside of it, but how Garder would twist it.

On the fourth day of the trial, she brought it before the jury and I drank the magick in like a sponge. Garder had no idea what she was dealing with. Or who.

Chapter Thirty One

JOURNAL

After nine months without Morgan, her magick drifted over me like lake water on a sweltering summer day. It was as potent as it had ever been and my fingers itched to reach out to the book Garder handled so casually. If she could feel what was pulsing from between those pages, she wouldn't be so cavalier.

As it was, her ignorance kept her turning pages until they came to one that was marked. Then she read, "'March twenty-third. My time is ending. I saw it in her eyes as the moon passed its crest in the sky. When she looked at me, her intent was clear. She has the knowledge now, and I am of no more use here. Soon, I will belong to another world.'"

Garder's eyes raised to the jury as she lowered the book. "Morgan LeFayette wrote these words. In them you can see how she regarded her life as coming to an end. Not a natural or willing end, but one with the intent of a determined young woman behind it. Ms. LeFayette states, 'I am of no more use here.' Now who would think that of her? Who would think to take this woman's knowledge into themselves and then disregard her as of no further use? There was only one such being to whom Ms. LeFayette had paid such particular attention. Alexandria Ryder was the one being to have such constant and familiar contact with the victim. Are we to believe that the woman she speaks of is any other but the Defendant? I think not."

My teeth set on edge and it took all I had not to correct her. At the same time, my fury at Morgan rippled out of me in waves that lapped at the ankles of all those around me–until Sarah gave a subtle kick to my own. Reining it in, I forced myself not to glare as she read from a few more passages. Each one hinted at my growing abilities, and a few were more disheartening as it was obvious Morgan was hiding things from me-though Garder made it sound as if *she* were hiding from me.

I pulsed and shook and seethed through an entire day of Garder making false assumptions about Morgan's intent in the passages she wrote. Then she reached the last passage and I felt my body grow cold.

"'It is almost done now. I can feel the days coming to a close. Another day and I will be down to hours. The oleander is more potent than I expected, but with the skill and care put into it, I could not expect anything less. It is a regret that I will not be able to see all those I care about, yet I suppose there is nothing left to be said that they do not already know.'"

Once more, Garder raised her eyes to the jury as she closed the book. "This woman knew she was being poisoned. Why did she do nothing to stop it? She knew who was responsible for her demise, yet she continued to feign ignorance. How come? Could it be that she looked at the younger woman sitting before you and felt fear tremble down into her bones? I don't think so. I believe, instead, that Ms. LeFayette loved Miss Ryder. Loved her enough that she wanted no harm to come to her. Indeed, her will suggests that she had every interest secured in taking care of her. So then why did Alexandria Ryder coldly, callously, and willfully poison her mentor? The answer is simple: greed. Why wait for tomorrow what could be had today?

"We have presented the evidence to you and explained the facts behind each one. And in the victim's own words, you've heard the chilling details of how an old woman was manipulated and killed by a compassionless teenager who thought only of her own gain. As I have asked of you from the beginning: we seek justice for these heinous crimes. Believing we have given you the means to provide it, the Prosecution rests."

A moment later, the court recessed until the following morning. Sarah gave me a knowing look and I nodded, more than ready to get on with my side of the whole ordeal. Though Morgan had taught me never to flout my magick, I was beginning to believe that the courtroom was about to have an experience it would never be able to believe.

"Now we've come full circle," I stated in a calm tone. In three days, I had given the jury most of the past year of my life. Each time, getting up on the stand was a little easier. A little harder. Yet, more rewarding.

Over the past few days, the feel of the jury had shifted. Their skepticism was still high, but so was their respect for what I could do. After all, these were all residents of Cedar Creek. On some level, almost all of them believed in witches and in magick. Even when they didn't want to admit it. Which was why they had come close to believing me.

They would need more than just my testimony, however. That's where I had to trust Sarah to see me through this. Because we would need to be able to prove Morgan's death was a suicide. Beyond any doubt.

"That is quite the story, Miss Ryder. And when, exactly, did you come under Ms. LeFayette's tutelage?" Sarah inquired.

"When I was nine."

"So, you knew her for four years?"

"Yes."

Sarah turned back to the jury as she responded, "Quite long enough not to be considered strangers anymore. Tell me, Miss Ryder, did you love my mother?"

There was a collective gasp as that knowledge circulated throughout the room. I glanced askance at the jurors to watch their eyes grow wide. Then the question began to sink in: Why would the victim's daughter defend her alleged murderer?

"More than you will ever know."

"Would you have ever hurt her?"

"No."

"Why should we believe you?" she challenged.

"There is nothing I can say that will make you believe me. But I loved Morgan and I respected her. She was my family."

Sarah smiled at me and nodded once. "I believe you," she announced.

After a pause, she turned to the table holding the evidence. My heart jumped as she picked up the journal. Turning to me, she cradled the little black book to her chest.

"How familiar are you with this book, Miss Ryder?"

I shook my head. "I'm not. Morgan never showed it to me."

"She didn't keep it with her other journals or her Book of Shadows?"

"No. I studied those too much. She never left it where I could read it."

Sarah turned to the jury. "At the time the Prosecution came into possession of this journal, there were only two sets of prints on it. One belonged to Morgan LeFayette. The other ... was mine."

"Objection, Your Honor. That cannot be verified."

Sarah strode back to our table and pulled a file out of her briefcase. "These are the lab results of a fingerprint analysis conducted on the journal last October. At the time, the only fingerprints found were those of Morgan LeFayette."

First, she showed the results to the judge before she passed them to the Prosecutor. While Garder's eyes widened, the judge asked, "And how did your fingerprints get to be on the evidence, Ms. Thompson?"

"At the time, the journal was not evidence, Your Honor. It was a memento, sent from mother to daughter. After I had the test conducted, I read it. Then I read it again and again."

"Then how did it come to be in the hands of the Prosecution?" he demanded.

"I sent it to them. It was my hope that they would read it and come to understand that my mother was an ill woman who was tired of living. She took her own life, only when she was sure Alexandria Ryder was ready to go on without her. If you will permit me, I would like to prove that to yourself and the members of the jury."

The judge gave a grave nod. "Very well. Objection overruled."

Turning back to me, Sarah stepped forward with Morgan's journal held to her chest once more. "Miss Ryder, did my mother ever discuss with you any health conditions she may have had?"

I shook my head. "No."

"Did you ever accompany her to an appointment or stress tests?"

"No. I don't even know when she would have gone to one. Morgan was a hermit."

Sarah nodded. "To many, it would appear she was." Then she opened the book to another marked passage and passed it to me. "Could you please read the passage for the date of January sixth?"

As soon as the book was in my hands, a jolt of energy shot up my arms, coalescing beneath the scar left by the lightning. For a moment, I lost my breath and it was hard to focus on what Sarah wanted me to do. At last, I shook my head a little and began to read.

Sarah had me read several passages. All with the same type of content. Things which Morgan had hidden very well from me.

As it happened, January sixth was when Morgan suffered from her first heart attack. At first, she didn't seem to know what it was. She drank some tea to help with the aches and went to sleep. Then it happened again a month later. That time, she'd done more than drink tea, she'd read up on her symptoms from the limited texts of her bookshelf. Her intuition had always been strong and she knew then what was happening to her.

The third one happened a week after the second and she took herself to the hospital for tests. It took a few days for the results to come back, but when they did, they confirmed her suspicions. Morgan was then diagnosed with cardiac ischemia, where the arteries to the heart became narrow and allowed less blood flow and oxygen to reach the heart, which caused her heart attacks.

From that point on, Morgan treated herself as only a witch of her caliber could. Yet, it wasn't enough. She continued to have heart attacks, although none of them were major enough to kill her. Though she knew that was only a matter of time.

Then came the passage concerning my vision-the first part of which the Prosecution had left out-where she describes what she saw at the same time that I saw my Ascension. Morgan knew she was going to die within the year, and she maintained her heart regiment only in the hopes of seeing my education to completion. When she learned that I would Ascend, she also knew the date she would be able to release herself.

The journal didn't describe *all* of that, of course. Else even the detectives would have let it drop. Yet, the implication was there through it all. Only a fool-or someone determined to ruin the life of someone else-could ignore that.

With the book in my hands, however, every impression it carried leapt out of its leather binding and seeped into my heart and mind. I began to cry the moment I realized Morgan began slow-dosing herself with the oleander so that she could have time. She wanted her heart to build up a measure of resistance to the poison so that she could say goodbye to me when the time came, instead of forcing her to miss my Ascension entirely.

I could have killed her.

Chapter Thirty Two

LETTER

Despite the magick pulsing from the book that I hadn't been allowed to examine yet, Sarah turned to Garder and turned me over to her. For a minute, Garder sat in her chair and said nothing while Sarah resumed her seat. Before my testimony, I knew Garder had been well prepared for cross-examination. After Sarah had me read about Morgan's medical problems however, she needed to change up her game plan.

For a few more seconds, she seemed to deliberate silently. During which time, I turned the book to the back cover, running my hand over an odd crease. The spell on the book pulsed from there, the seal impossible to break except by magick.

I was engrossed in my study when Garder's

words managed to penetrate. Across the room, she lifted her head to study the judge. "I would like to request a recess until tomorrow, Your Honor."

My head twitched at her words, noting somewhere in my subconscious that it was already four in the afternoon and that stopping at that point wasn't a bad idea. Something the judge must have reasoned, himself, because he then announced, "Court will recess until tomorrow morning at eight."

Before he could say anything else, my head snapped up and I looked up at him. "Can I open this first?" I asked. If I had to wait on Garder to cross examine me, I knew that I wouldn't get that journal back in my hands until Sarah allowed it.

The judge paused in the act of picking up his gavel. Curious, he leaned toward me. "Open what?"

"The folder at the back. Cheap journals like these have folders in the back, but Morgan sealed this one. Can I open it?"

Without answering, the judge held out his hand for the journal. His thick brows furrowed as he ran a hand along the crease, examining the book from the top so that he could see the same raised portion that I had found. Just as if someone had folded a sheet of paper and tucked it inside. Perhaps what was just as damning was the fact that the last page that Morgan would have written on-near the three-quarter mark of the book-was cut out of the journal.

With a look, the judge summoned Sarah to the bench. She approached with a confident gait that made me think she'd set us up. The apple hadn't fallen far from the tree in her case.

"What do you make of this?" the judge demanded as Garder approached on the other side of Sarah.

Taking the journal from him, Sarah gave it the same examination that we had, but for a far shorter period of time. In a casual voice, she stated, "The missing page appears to be sealed within this envelope in the back. But I am unable to open it. Care to try?" she asked, handing the journal to Garder.

The Prosecutor schooled her expression as she took the journal from her. For several minutes, she attempted to pry at any loose piece of the stiff paper, but it wouldn't come loose. At last, she handed the book back to Sarah with an imperious remark, "It seems to be the back cover. Nothing more."

Casual as could be, Sarah passed the journal back to me. Without waiting for permission, I ran a finger over the sealed portion, pouring my intent into the magick kept there. The stiff back parted as soon as I took my finger away.

Eager as I was, I didn't bother with anyone else's reactions as I pulled free the missing page. Opening it, my eyes scoured over the familiar handwriting and a lump lodged itself in my throat. Tears built within my eyes and I could barely read the last words. As soon as I could, I thrust the note at Sarah and tried to get myself under control.

While I was wiping my eyes, I heard Sarah take a deep breath before she passed the note to Garder. My vision was clear enough to see her face grow pale as she read the words. Then she passed it to the judge. At last, he passed it back to Sarah and asked her to read it for the court. Instead of complying, Sarah held the letter out to me.

"Read it, Alex. It's for you."

Taking a breath, I nodded. My hands shook a little as I took the note back. In an instant, my hand shot to my eyes as the words stabbed at my heart again and again.

Dearest Alexandria,

I am sorry.

It seems an innocuous phrase, but I do mean it to the depths of my soul. I apologize for what pain and confusion you are now enduring because of my actions. It was never my intent that you should be harmed, but this cannot be avoided. Thus, I shall do my best to clear some of your confusion, and hopefully give you some peace.

I am dying, Alexandria. My heart has been failing me for some months, and I feel myself as less part of this world each day. Soon, it shall give out entirely.

There have been steps made to prevent this, but they are a temporary balm. My end is near, and I had feared that it would reach me before you were ready for it.

Then you became aware of how soon your

Ascension would take place and I knew that the Goddess was taking pity upon me. With as much as you have come to know, the things left for you to learn is what experience alone can teach. I am of no more use to you, Alexandria, and thus I am preparing myself and my body to succumb to the great sleep of this life.

I would ask you not to mourn if I thought it would do me any good. Thus I shall not ask for your forgiveness either. Know that I love you, Alexandria, and you are a great comfort to me. Now I will give unto you all of the blessings of which I am capable. You have earned them.

Love,
Morgan

I was crying by the time I finished speaking. Sarah was forced to take the letter from me and divulge the last paragraph to the jury, because I couldn't speak clearly enough to do it myself. When she finished, a long, heavy silence filled the courtroom.

At last, Sarah turned to the judge. "If it is at all possible, Your Honor, I believe myself and the Prosecutor would like a private word in your chambers."

The judge nodded and a flurry of motion broke through the stillness. I was escorted out of the courtroom to a holding area while the jury was taken and put into theirs. Since the judge had called an hour long recess, everyone else gathered their things and it seemed like most were going to get an early dinner.

I waited in the holding area for forty minutes before Sarah found me. The smile on her face was beautiful to behold as she took a seat next to me. It was the first time Sarah ever hugged me.

"They've authenticated the note and the judge has allowed for me to petition for dismissal. The DA's office have agreed and now we're just waiting to go back inside and make it official."

"It's over?" I whispered, unable to speak any louder. "I can go home?"

"It's over," she agreed. "You can go home."

I threw my arms around her and didn't let go until we were forced to go back into the courtroom.

From there, everything was a blur. Voices came to me as if through a tunnel as the formalities were gotten over. Then I was being grabbed and hugged by everyone near me. For the news reporters, it seemed more than a little odd when there was no grieving family torn up by the results, because they were busy squeezing the life out of me and crying with relief.

At first, I felt like I was being mauled by parents. My mom grabbed me up first, but then my dad snatched me from her. Anne was more patient as she eased me out of his grip. Then I hugged Sarah again while the tears were coming out of my eyes. When I turned around, Nathan was standing there, grinning at me. A second later, his arms had encircled my waist and he spun me around, both of us laughing with relief and joy.

And it was a relief. For all of us. The minute the dismissal was announced, we'd all reversed in age by about five years. It made us absolutely giddy. Thus, we were a happy, laughing mass of people as we spilled out of the courthouse. Flanked by my dad and Sarah, I stopped on the wide steps and delivered a statement Morgan would have been proud of.

Sarah said that maybe it was my job to teach

the people of Cedar Creek not to make assumptions. To teach them that being different was no excuse for being treated in this way. That my magick shouldn't make me a target for false accusations, but a being who had just a bit better insight into how the world worked. Maybe she was right, and maybe they would listen. One could only hope.

Chapter Thirty Three

BURIED TREASURE

Nathan and I spent two days closing up the cottage. Anne wanted to help, but I think she realized that this was something we needed to do. After a thorough cleaning, plumbing problem preventatives, and turning off the electricity and heat, the only thing left was security. Which was why I needed Nathan.

It started off with a simple smudge of the house, burning sage and cedar to purify and protect the cottage. Afterward, I threw a layer of every warding spell I knew around the cottage and the garden. Nathan had to be present so that I could incorporate him into the spells, so that the house would recognize him as a caretaker. If I hadn't added him in, then even he would not get past the barriers.

For the rest of the property, I added more general warding spells. Though the reputation of the grove would probably have served to keep the more superstitious away, I wasn't allowing anyone with harmful or malignant intent anywhere near the woods. Yet, people who wanted to take a casual stroll or just felt drawn to the trees would find themselves safely sheltered.

The lake I left open. If it weren't for that place, I would never have met Morgan. Nathan and I would never have become friends. As far as my young life went, that lake was a massive part of it. If anyone else needed a place like that, I wasn't going to deprive them of it.

As soon as I finished, I turned to Nathan. His sad smile said he already knew. Turning toward the door, he called back over his shoulder, "I'll see you at the lake."

I nodded until he closed the door behind him. Then I took a deep breath and turned to stare at the cottage. Morgan's cottage. No matter what the little piece of paper said, this place would always be hers. Despite the centuries of witches and women who called this place home, it could belong to no one else.

It was time to say goodbye.

The heaviness of that admission settled around my heart and I could feel myself cracking. Like a mirror, the breaks kept spreading, pieces fell away, littering everything around me. Important pieces. What was worse, was that I knew the tiny pieces were nothing compared to the huge chunks of me I was about to lose. And when we finally left Cedar Creek, I wouldn't be the Alexandria Ryder anyone knew.

A sob fell into the silence and I eased my way to the polished wooden floor. Folding in on myself, I pressed my forehead to my knees and allowed myself to break. Just this once, I could cry for everything I was losing. Everything I had lost.

For almost an hour, I couldn't raise myself from that floor. Though I pushed and I shoved at my own defeat, it weighed me down like an anchor. The memories from the house pressed in on me and held me in place, determined not to let me go. At last, however, I felt a faint shift. The turning of an hourglass.

With the tears under control, at least, I rose

to my feet and took a long, heavy breath. For one minute, I closed my eyes. When I opened them, Morgan's urn was setting on the heavy wooden table. As if in answer to a question, I nodded my head and scooped it up. Then I walked out the door without daring to look back.

Each step I took toward the circle was an exercise in determination. Magick thrummed through the earth beneath my feet and it tugged me along. A good thing, too, or I wasn't sure I'd have had it in me to approach the site of Morgan's demise. Though I'd returned to the circle for most of the holidays of my faith, it was a different thing when I was bringing Morgan back to it.

The moment it came into view, I felt it steal my breath. With the spring sprinting toward summer, it was full of energy and magick. Its protective shield rippled as a steady breeze got caught in the web before spiriting itself away in a playful dance. And as I neared it, a joyous thrum bounded out of it as if it were happy to see me.

Despite what I had just endured, a laugh escaped me. Blasted with the magick of the circle in such a festive state, I couldn't help but feel my heart lighten a bit. Then another wave hit me and I was reminded that there was an effect for every cause. For the circle, the passing of one season to the next was cause for celebration. The effect being the lightening of my mood.

By the time I had reached the center, I no longer felt the melancholy of what I was about to do. This was the type of welcome Morgan would have loved. One full of joy and love. I broke the seal on the top of the urn and cast her ashes to the wind. An instant later, she was carried around the circle, coating every rock and blade of grass, before the remaining ashes got caught in the shield. That's where she stayed. To protect and watch over the circle, as was her sacred charge.

For one, endless moment, I was surrounded by her. Caressed by her compassion and caring for me. Teased and challenged as only she was capable of. And I was reminded again of her love for me and how infinite it was.

As I was leaving, I bottled that feeling up inside of me like ocean sand in a thick glass vial. If ever I needed a dose, I could always just tease out the cork and get a quick whiff of ocean breeze before bottling away my treasure once more. With the months to come, I had a good idea of how precious it would become.

Taking one more deep breath before I lost sight of the circle, I closed my eyes and willed myself to be at the lake. When I opened them, Matt and Nathan were sitting on either end of the log. Nathan paused mid-sentence and turned to me, his eyes scrutinizing my face, searching for the grief that I was unable to feel in that moment. Ignoring his questioning expression, I bounded over the log and grinned at the boys as I sat down.

We sat there and talked for a long time. None of us wanted to leave, because none of us wanted to say goodbye. After all we had been through together, separation seemed nigh a sin in our minds. In the end, it wasn't up to us.

A few hours before sunset, the three of us began the long walk up Old Grove Road. For a while, even Matt had adopted our customary code of silence. Yet, with each step, I could feel the levity leaving me and I fought back against the tears that threatened to build in my eyes. But there was no way for me to say goodbye to my only friends and not want to cry.

As we neared the end, Matt finally got up the nerve to ask, "When do you leave?"

"Eight o'clock tomorrow morning," I sighed.

"You gonna have time to say goodbye?"

My lungs constricted. "No. That's what today is for."

Our feet had just reached Norfolk Street and he took a deep breath before releasing it slowly. Then he turned to me and forced a half-smile. "Guess this is goodbye then."

I nodded, stepping into the hug he offered. Neither of us was naïve. Our chances of seeing one another again had almost vanished the moment my dad announced that we were moving. I was fourteen and he was almost sixteen. This year of his life could fade and he could forget all about the witch he used to date. He, at least, had that option. I wouldn't fault him if he took it.

Several minutes later, Matt let me go. He stepped back as if he were forcing himself to do it and kept his face averted when I tried to get a good look at it.

"Bye, Lex," he muttered one last time before turning and darting across the street.

"Bye, Matt," I whispered back as he disappeared from view. Then I turned to look at Nathan, my eyes full of tears.

He didn't say anything. Instead, he took one of my hands in his and turned left, heading for my house. We didn't speak as we continued our walk, though sometimes my thoughts made me grip tighter to his hand than I should have. Despite my fierce battle, a few tears made their way silently down my face. All of my contentment from earlier was gone. Now, I was standing on a precipice, waiting for the inevitable fall.

That end was just over the horizon and neither of us wanted to greet it any faster. Instead, we dragged our feet the moment we turned onto Verity Lane. It would take prep work to make us say goodbye, and I knew the only reason I would be able to get through it was because I knew it was temporary.

I would see Nathan again. When I came home to Cedar Creek, I knew he would be here. And I knew that nothing could happen between now and then that would change our friendship. Nathan would always have my back, and I would always have his.

With that knowledge hidden within the

ocean vial of my thoughts, I treated it as the buried treasure that it was. Every time missing home became unbearable, I would get a glimpse of what waited for me here. Knowing that, I would be able to get through anything.

At last, we reached the gate in front of my house and stopped. Turning to face him, the silence lengthened as our eyes drank in the last sight we would have of one another for years to come. When my eyes raised to his, they flickered back toward the house.

"I can't imagine Cedar Creek without you, Lex."

It was hard to capture his gaze with my own, but when I did I found my own sadness in his eyes. My own memories. My own heartache.

"And I can't imagine leaving. This is my home, Nathan." With that, the dam broke and the tears started to course down my face in a relentless river.

Nathan reached out and pulled me to him. I buried my face against his shoulder and he squeezed me tighter. Except for my gasps of breath, silence reigned between us. As it always had.

There came a time, however, when I could feel that the separation was occurring. It was a sense of stepping back and knowing that it was now or never. If I didn't let him go in that moment, I would never be capable of it.

Nathan chose that moment to whisper in my ear, "I'll miss you, Lex. Every day."

My throat tightened. "I'll miss you, too. Every single day, Nathan."

Then I pulled back just far enough so I could meet his gaze. As my thoughts got lost in those emerald pools, I reminded myself that this would not be the last time I saw them. I would come home. To Cedar Creek and to Nathan. Nothing would stand in my way.

At last, I closed my eyes. Nathan stepped out of my arms and I tried to drown out the sound of him leaving. Turning toward the gate, I didn't open my eyes again until I was sure he was out of sight. Until that moment, it felt as if my heart wasn't able to break any more than it had already been broken.

It felt as if I had just let go of everything that was holding me together.

Raising my eyes to the house, it took a few

seconds before I could see more than a blur of red brick and ivy. When at last the colonial door, crown of chimneys, and casement windows came into focus, I could feel the nostalgia rise up inside of me.

This is how a house in New England should look.

That was how I left my last goodbye.

ACKNOWLEDGEMENTS

I always think of acknowledgements as the hardest part of writing a book. A lot goes into the process, and if you don't have incredible people to back you through it all, things can get stressful. I'm grateful for all of the people that help me as a person, as well as a writer.

I have to start with my best friend, Chrissy. This is my Wonder Woman and the whole reason my books have ever seen print. She's a formatter, designer, part-time editor, and full-time encourager. Every single day, this woman impresses me. Never more so than when she takes time out of her schooling, her jobs, or her life to help me make my dreams a reality. I worship the ground she walks on.

I would also like to thank my friend Mandy for being a book bully. Being forced to read a book your friend is fanatic about is never a bad thing. Buying four copies and shipping them to your friends goes above and beyond anyone's expectations. Thank you, Mandy, for always pushing me to keep my dreams alive.

As always, I have to thank my sister, Mariah. Without her, I don't know if this series would have ever been completed. Her enthusiasm for this story continues to fuel my pride in it. Thank you so much, sister.

I'd also like to thank my other siblings, sibling-in-laws, and the nieces and nephews I was able to get out of the deal. I love you all so much. (Mostly the kiddos, not gonna lie.) Thank you all for being part of my life, even though we're far apart.

My significant other, Christopher, puts up with so much from me. Too many late nights of ignoring him, dishes, vacuuming, etc... Where was I going with this? Oh yeah, I love you, honey! Thank you for knowing when to leave me alone to deal with all the people in my head, and also when to pull me back into reality.

Of course, I also have to thank my Nana and Papa. As with any book I write, I know it all started with their encouragement, support, and love. Without them, I wouldn't have known that I had the kind of potential and determination it took to turn a hobby into a craft that truly defines me.

To wrap this up, I have to thank my Big Dude. No one could mean more to me than you. I'm so happy to have you as my mom, and I can't imagine my life without you. Everything I accomplish in this life is because of everything you've done for me.

ABOUT THE AUTHOR

Hollow Ryan is a Michigan native with thirty years spent too much in her own head, and twenty years putting it all on paper. This obsession with the written word has led her to publish the five-book paranormal series, *The Prideful Magick Collection*. It has also started her on a journey full of *Demon Kin*.

When not working on her ever-expanding Work List, Hollow is dealing with the three most spoiled fur-children to be found in Northeastern Michigan. (Her spouse is absolutely to blame for that.)

For more information, please visit:
www.hollowryan.com

Read on for a look at...

Valerian

PRIDEFUL MAGICK COLLECTION
BOOK THREE

Chapter One

SCARS

One day, I would pay the balance for the damage done. When I was done inflicting it.

Every scar marked a day that I would atone for. Four hundred and twenty-seven had come to pass.

It wasn't that I wanted to hurt myself. I needed to. More than the compulsion and routine, I burned so that I would *feel* something again. Anything.

Midnight struck and I took a deep breath while I held my left arm out in front of me. Staring at a spot just above my elbow, I released the magick in a familiar spell that brought to me the delicious pain that I deserved. Pain that I had earned. Soon, the skin transformed into an angry red as the heat seared it from within.

As the design began to form, the burning started to feel more like acid, causing me to clench my teeth against a scream. My right hand curled into a fist and I began to pound on my thigh. At the same time, my left arm tensed, the agony shooting along the nerves all the way up into my shoulder. It coalesced in the star-shaped scar over my left breast before bursting forth and blazing down my arm once more in the last brutal second of completion.

At last, I was able to throw my head back and take in ragged gasps of air while the heat began to subside. Pain still pulsed in the skin, but it was fading into a throbbing ache rather than searing torment. With the same pace, the redness began to fade, leaving a raised white scar where the skin had been smooth a moment ago.

When my heart rate fell into a more natural rhythm, I lowered my head to stare at the new addition. The oak leaf was fitted in amongst the hundreds of ivy leaves that coated my upper arm. One other oak leaf rested near the top of my shoulder, marking the anniversary of my first trip down Old Grove Road. In two more days, I would add my second apple blossom for the day that I met my beloved mentor, Morgan LeFayette.

My eyes closed as the memories attempted to resurface. It wasn't hard, now, to push them back. Not like it was at first. On certain days, however, I let them come.

Somewhere behind that black wall in my mind, I found myself back on the old dirt road. Oak trees stood as sentinels, lining either side of the road at equal spaces. Between them, the young trees and ferns grew up with a surprising rapidity. A playful breeze tossed the leaves, sending up the scent of mint from the scrubby plants that lined part of the road. It was a fantasy of mine that promised tranquility.

One that was ripped away the moment I pictured my two best friends standing in the middle of Old Grove Road. Nathan Richards and Matthew Graham. One who I revealed was my mentor's grandson, and the other who'd been my first boyfriend. Nathan and I had sat side by side on a school bus and in class for four years without really talking. Still, we knew we were there for each other. And Matt had been the first person in Cedar Creek to be interested in me in a personal manner. It was part of my greatest heartbreak, having to leave them both behind. Of all the people to know what I was capable of, Nathan was the most aware of my abilities.

As I thought about him, the first of my scars began to warm and I rubbed at it through my shirt. Unlike the other ivy leaves, the most important ones spread from my left breast, across my collarbone, and merged into the pattern of my left arm. The first was created beside the star-shaped scar left by a lightning strike on the day of my Ascension, right before Morgan committed suicide.

Of all the days that could have caused everything in me to snap, I might have thought that would be it. It wasn't. Not until the day I left Cedar Creek did I feel like everything that made me *me* was chipped away. My compassion, forgiveness, honesty, and hope withered away beneath the harsh glare of my reality. Worse than that, a fierce wind came along and tore my pride, honor, and confidence out of my grasp. When I was uprooted, I had but self-loathing and wrath to cling to.

And I had used them.

To most people, the scars in my arm would be the equivalent to cutting. It offered me the control I was lacking in my life. Using my magick to hurt myself seemed like an unfathomable cry for help. And using my magick to hide it helped me to deal with the shame of having done it in the first place.

Yet, my scars were more than that. Each one created at midnight, marking every day that I spent away from my real home. They were my calendar. Sands in an hourglass, keeping track of the passage of time.